James Clegg

**Extracts from the Diary and Autobiography of the Rev.**

**James Clegg,**

Nonconformist Minister and Doctor of Medicine, A.D. 1679 to 1755

James Clegg

**Extracts from the Diary and Autobiography of the Rev. James Clegg,**
*Nonconformist Minister and Doctor of Medicine, A.D. 1679 to 1755*

ISBN/EAN: 9783337013400

Printed in Europe, USA, Canada, Australia, Japan

Cover: Foto ©Raphael Reischuk / pixelio.de

More available books at **www.hansebooks.com**

CHINLEY CHAPEL.

# EXTRACTS

FROM THE

# DIARY AND AUTOBIOGRAPHY

OF THE

# REV. JAMES CLEGG,

Nonconformist Minister and Doctor of Medicine,
A.D. 1679 to 1755.

---

EDITED,

With Explanatory Notes and Introductory Chapter,

BY

## HENRY KIRKE, M.A., B.C.L., Oxon.,

*Author of "The First English Conquest of Canada;" "Twenty-five Years in British Guiana;" &c., &c.*

---

BUXTON:
C. F. WARDLEY, "HIGH PEAK NEWS" OFFICES, MARKET PLACE.
LONDON:
SAMPSON LOW, MARSTON, AND COMPANY, LIMITED.

1899.

# PREFACE.

Dr. Clegg's Diary is in the possession of Mr. W. H. Greaves-Bagshawe, of Ford Hall, near Chapel-en-le-Frith, a great-great-great nephew of the Mr. Bagshawe, of Ford, who is so often mentioned in its pages. I am indebted to Mr. Bagshawe for permission to publish the Diary, and also for some valuable information which has been included in my Notes.    H.K.

# INTRODUCTORY CHAPTER.

The M.S. from which the following extracts are taken is contained in a folio book of 265 pages, written on rough paper, and with ink which in some places has faded almost to obscurity. The leaves of the book have been reverently repaired by its present possessor, but in some places even his care has failed to recover certain entries which have become undecipherable. The writing is small and cramped, and each page is divided into two columns, each column containing about 800 words, so the length of the whole is considerable. The entries seem to have been made almost daily, except when the worthy Doctor was on his travels, when they were written up immediately after his return.

This M.S. is the record of a life; a carefully kept Diary written up with scrupulous care and honesty, wherein are set down the most trivial details and the most serious occurrences, together with expressions of hope and fear, personal confessions, and words of supplication and thanksgiving;—the varied outcome of an educated, active and pious mind. The whole, as might be expected, is intensely devout, filled to overflowing with the spirit of true religion. In this daily record the writer stands vividly revealed; he hides nothing, he lays his soul bare; not only are his actions detailed, but his motives, his thoughts, his temptations and his sins are all displayed. It is an intensely human document.

Who and what sort of man the Revd. Dr. Clegg was will be sufficiently revealed in the extracts themselves. What is here printed is but an infinitesimal amount of the whole Diary; the greater part of the entries are of a nature wholly uninteresting to the general reader, and consist principally of daily visits to the sick, the poor and the needy, the fatherless and widow; long details of illnesses told in the plainest language, not suitable to the ideas of modern delicacy; details of sermons preached, of the common incidents of farm life and ministerial business, of numerous funerals, with the inevitable sermons setting forth to his or her weeping friends the virtues of the departed; quarrels amongst neighbours arranged, in which he ever appeared as a peacemaker; family incidents, a meteorological journal, and a general gazette of all the births, marriages and deaths in the village where he lived and for miles around.

Many of my readers may think that the extracts are too many as they stand, but as many a commonplace wall or building loses by degrees its ugliness, and under the softening hand of time, becomes a thing of beauty, covered with green moss and grey lichen, wall-flowers and stonecrop, so these commonplace entries seem through the lapse of time to have acquired an interest not their own, full as they are of quaintness and old-world savour; it would seem also desirable to show the writer in all his aspects, and most men's lives are after all made up of apparently trivial details, the great events being few and far between.

One is struck in reading Dr. Clegg's Diary by the wonderful energy of the man—as healer of bodies as well as souls his labour was continuous. After a week of toil, we find him every Sunday preaching twice and catechising 30 or 40 children between the services. And these sermons were no elegant little discourses turned off in 15 or 20 minutes, for we often read that he was in the pulpit for three hours at a stretch, and once he mentions three hours and three quarters as the period of his discourse.

His visiting was remarkable.—To seven or eight houses situated miles apart he is in one day a welcome guest; the Squire in his hall, the Yeoman at his homestead, the poor woman in her cottage are all equally favoured by his attentions. Wherever any-one is sick, he is to be found; he is praying by the bedsides of the dying, he is reading the services of the dead at every grave; the poor never leave him empty; the wretched in mind turn to him for consolation, and the distressed for assistance. Preaching, praying, healing the sick, helping the needy, allaying strife, re-buking sin, this worthy pastor pursues his Christ-like life—surely an example to us that is worth preserving and studying.

Nor was Dr. Clegg a sour ascetic: frequent in his diary are references to "innocent recreation." He joined his friends in fish-ing and coursing, played a game at bowls or shovel-board, spent a festive evening in a tavern, and even allowed his friends and relations to go to the Races without rebuke. His charity was great: when he was too ill to conduct service in his own Chapel, he advised his family to go to Church; when in Manchester he attended morning prayers in the Collegiate Church; he dined with Vicars and Rectors, and welcomed the itinerant Methodist preacher, until he found the latter falling into the sin of Antino-mianism when he withstood him to the face. He is ever ready to do battle for the faith that is in him, whether his adversary be a Papist or a Socinian.

But what strikes the reader of his Diary more than anything else is his childlike piety and humility, and absolute dependence on God for everything, and his recognition of God's providence in all things, even the most trivial incidents of life. To him God is no mere abstraction, He is ever-present, the Omnipotent in small things as in great. Such texts as "Behold the very hairs of your head are all numbered" and "Not a sparrow falleth to the ground without your Father" were by him construed literally and absolutely. In everything he does, whether he be carting hay, cutting down trees, transacting business, preaching or praying, administering medicine, travelling or visiting, or, even taking shares in a lottery, he sees the over-ruling hand of Providence, guiding, restraining, protecting. If he falls from his horse, his safety is due to God's protection; if the weather be fine for his haymaking it is owing to God's goodness; if his medicines operate successfully it is God's work; and that not generally, but particularly, in each individual case. He is mighty in prayer, he prays without ceasing, he prays with his patients and has more faith in his prayers than in his medicines; he prays for his children, for himself, or the nation; he fills every house he enters with prayer and supplication, and that not formally as of duty, but with a thorough conviction of their efficacy. When he hears of a neighbour in grievous peril, he goes up to his closet, and there prays privately for her individually, and when she is relieved soon afterwards, he attributes her recovery to God's answer to his supplications. There is not the slightest tinge of hypocrisy in the man, he is guileless and transparent, conscious of his own weaknesses and shortcomings, but strong in his never-failing faith and dependence on God's protecting care.

Such a character as Clegg's is an interesting study in these days. Not that he stood alone; there were hundreds of devout men in his time, and there have been thousands since, who have held the same views, led similar lives, being monuments of faith and piety. But there is something peculiarly interesting in Dr. Clegg's life; his dual position as pastor and doctor, the transitional period in which he lived, far removed from the old days, but without the fulness of modern life; the stress and toil of existence in the High Peak, which was one of the last parts of England to assimilate itself to modern ideas and customs, all combine to give a peculiar colouring to his ministrations.

Dr. Clegg's position as a medical man gave him particular advantages. He appears to have been the only doctor in the parish, and his fame and practise spread far beyond its limits. In his Diary we find frequent visits in his medical capacity, and in reference to urgent appeals, to Buxton, Tideswell, Congleton, Leek, Macclesfield, Derby, Chesterfield, and Gainsborough, and wherever he goes, to Ordinations, double Lectures, or other gatherings of ministers, his services are freely given to any and all persons who seek his aid, and we even find him carrying help and comfort to those that were in prison. Many persons who must have rejected his views as a pastor were glad to avail themselves of his medical skill, so he was a welcome guest in many a Rectory and Parsonage which would otherwise have been closed against him.

As one of the earliest Nonconformist divines it is interesting to discover how he entered the ministry, under what auspices and by what authority. Dr. Clegg seems to have been naturally of a serious disposition, and although in his youth led into evil which he afterwards deeply deplored, he never appears to have fallen into vulgar dissipation. As early as his 20th year he came under the influence of **Mr. Joseph Dawson**, of Rochdale, a serious Dissenting minister, who evidently turned the thoughts of his young disciple towards the ministry; indeed, Clegg preached his first sermon at Bispham before he was twenty-one. He continued to preach in divers places without any authority, and in July, 1703, he was called to preach an approbation sermon at Malcalf, near Chapel-en-le-Frith, in Derbyshire, to a congregation which had recently been deprived of its pastor, the celebrated " Apostle of the Peak," and, his discourse meeting with success, he was asked to remain. He accepted the offer, and found a home at Ford Hall, near Malcalf, as tutor to the sons of Mr. Samuel Bagshaw. Here he lived for some time, studying in Mr. Bagshaw's library, and also subscribing to the Mudie of the period and so obtaining all the new books. As he was not yet ordained, Clegg could not baptize nor administer the Lord's Supper, which disabilities were troublesome to his congregation; so, by the advice of Matthew Henry, he determined to seek Ordination, forwarded testimonials from his tutor, Mr. Charlton, to the ministers in Derbyshire, and was ordained at Malcalf by six of the principal pastors of the county and neighbourhood. The service adopted seems to have been as follows : One of the ministers preached, another prayed, then the candidate made a confession of faith, on which confession he was cross-examined by another minister. If his confession and answers were satisfactory he was set apart for the ministry by the laying on of hands by the ministers present, after which the oldest minister charged him as to his duties and responsibilities.

After his ordination Clegg entertained all the ministers and chief men of the congregation at dinner.

His stipend was not excessive, as it was but little over £20 per annum, so that when he married Miss Anne Champion, of Edale, and begat sons and daughters, he was obliged to take a farm at Stodhart, near Chapel-en-le-Frith, to enable him to maintain them. He resided at Stodhart Hall until his death in 1755. An attempt had been made soon after his marriage by his wife's relations, backed up by Mr. Cresswell, Vicar of Hope, to induce him to conform to the Anglican Church; he was offered a cure worth £40 or £50 per annum, but Clegg refused to desert his congregation, and the Vicar's arguments failed to persuade him.

There was no Medical Act in 1703, so there was nothing to prevent the Rev. James Clegg from doctoring himself and his congregation, if they would allow him; but he must in some way or other have acquired extensive medical knowledge, as he obtained a considerable local reputation as a physician and was called to sick beds in five neighbouring counties. But he himself felt that his position would be more secure and his reputation enhanced, if he could obtain 'recognition from some learned Society and receive the official seal which a medical degree can confer. With this view he wrote as follows to an old friend, Dr. Calamy : " Sept. 11th, 1728. Revd. and dear Sir, Soon after I came into the County I was advised by that Learned and worthy Gentleman Mr Saml Bagshaw of Ford (son of the Apostle of the Peak) to study Physick that I might be that way as well as the other serviceable to the poor in these parts many of whom he thought perished for want of a little seasonable help. This I was also much pressed to and assisted in, by Dr. Adam Holland of Macclesfield who very freely gave me the best advice he could whilst he lived, and left me all his manuscripts when he died. Some part of my time has been spent in this study for twenty years past in which time I have been looking into the most famous Authors I could compass ancient and modern, but never adventured to practise much except in ordinary cases and amongst the poorer sort, who have been very thankful, and that has been most of my reward. Of late I have been called in to some families of better note about us of different persuasions which has very much disturbed some zealots for the Church who now threaten me with a prosecution in the Spiritual Court for practising without a license. I am resolved rather to desist than apply to that Court, and yet would gladly be enabled to continue doing what I can for the good of my friends and neighbours every way.

Some of my brethren, as Mr. Dixon of Bolton and Mr. Lawrence of Newcastle have procured diplomas for the degree of Dr. from some of ye Universities in North Brittain. Some years ago I was advised to apply for one to Glasgow and some friends who were then students there offered me their interest and assistance, but I then declined it chiefly on account of ye cost, but now I am willing to strain to ye utmost of my ability rather than fall into ye hands of that greedy and merciless Court.

I know not any person in England that hath so great an interest in ye Universities of Edinburgh and Glasgow as your father, and I beg you will make use of your interest with him to prevail on him to direct and assist me in this affair. The state of my health and other circumstances will not permit me to undertake so long a journey at present, and I doubt not but his interest can procure me such a favour without my personal appearance; but perhaps some testimonial of my proficiency from some noted Physitians may be insisted on; as to which and ye fees I must pay, I desire to be instructed by you, by the first opportunity. I have a Brother-in-Law who deals in Manchester wares and visits Glasgow and Edinburgh thrice every year, and will do me all the service he can."

This application of his seems to have been partially successful, for although Edinburgh and Glasgow did not enrol him amongst their Doctors of Medicine, he received that degree from the University of Aberdeen, as we learn from an entry in his Diary.

" October 1729. Being this month created Doctor of Physick by a Diploma Medicum from the University of Aberdeen in North Brittain upon the Testimonials and Recommendations of Dr.

Nettleton of Halifax, Dr. Dixon of Bolton and Dr. Latham of Finderne I think it is now proper to keep a more exact account of my patients, their diseases, ye Remedies prescribed, and the event, depending above all things on the Divine blessing for success."

Chapel-en-le-Frith, where Dr. Clegg lived, is an ancient market town in the N.W. angle of Derbyshire, and has been until lately one of the most old-fashioned places in England. Situated in the High Peak, about 700 feet above sea level, and surrounded by hills rising to an elevation of 2000 feet, it enjoys a climate more famed for its bracing properties than its geniality. As its name indicates, it owes its origin to our Norman Conquerors, the whole district for miles around being in their time a vast forest, wherein wolves, bears, wild boars, deer, wild cats and martens were preserved for the amusement of our Norman Kings: it was the favourite hunting ground of the Plantagenets. The King's Castle in the High Peak (six miles from Chapel-en-le-Frith), was built by Wm. Peverel on the foundations of an earlier building of a Saxon monarch, and here all our Norman and Angevin Kings lodged whilst hunting in the Peak Forest.

The foresters and keepers of the King's game became so numerous that about the year 1220 they purchased land from Wm. de Ferrars (who after the disgrace of Peverel had obtained a grant of the High Peak Manor), and built thereon a Chapel for Divine worship which was called the Chapel in the Forest, and it was dedicated to that martyred Saint, Thomas a Becket, whose blood had been shed in Canterbury Cathedral about 50 years before.

In 1372 the Manor of the High Peak with its Castle and Forest was granted to John, Duke of Lancaster, and it has remained as part of the Duchy ever since. As the Regal power waned and our Kings and Royal Dukes were engaged in long and expensive wars with France and Scotland, or were fighting among themselves for Crown and lands, the oppressive Forest laws were gradually relaxed. As population increased encroachments were made on the Royal lands. The foresters of fee who had obtained grants of land for preserving the King's rights, encroached on the Forest, cutting down trees to build their homesteads, enclosing convenient patches of land, killing off wild beasts, and fencing in their flocks and herds. Richard le Savage, and a Peak lady, Philota de Kinder, obtained licenses from the King to kill all wolves, wild cats and bears within the forest bounds. As did their masters so did the freedmen, who dwelt around their lords' messuages.

Gradually the forest pure and simple receded until the wolves and other wild animals disappeared, and the land devoted to the deer became reduced to about a tenth of its former dimensions.

During the Wars of the Roses, when no man knew who might be his King to-morrow, the population within the Forest boundaries increased very largely, houses sprang up in all directions, lands were enclosed and roads made. Some faint efforts were made during the Tudor Monarchy to recover the rights of the King, but they were gone past recall; and under the Stuarts and the Commonwealth, they were dropped almost entirely. In the Civil Wars the last poor remnant of the deer were slain, and the Peak Forest as a place for the Chase passed away for ever.

From the foregoing it will be seen that the parish of Chapel-en-le-Frith was never, like so many English parishes, the property of one family. There was no Squire, no Rector; the freeholders of the parish, descendants of the old foresters, elected their own Chaplain, as they do now, and have done for 650 years. Several families of note lived in the parish whose sons were slain at Cressy, Agincourt, and Flodden (most of the archers who won the field of Agincourt came from Derbyshire and Nottinghamshire, the home of Robin Hood and Little John, the latter of whom lies buried within the bounds of the Peak Forest), but they have all with one exception died out and disappeared as landowners, although their names and no doubt numbers of their descendants are still to be found in the parish.*

When Dr. Clegg came to Malcalf, in 1702, Chapel-en-le-Frith must have been a populous place. All the principal farmhouses and residences in the parish were then built, most of them dating from the Tudor and Stuart periods. There were large stretches of common land still unenclosed, and the roads were mere bridle tracks winding over moors and wastes. No coaches nor carriages were used. All produce, even coals, was carried on pack horses, long strings of which were continually passing through the town from Sheffield and Chesterfield to Stockport and Manchester and back again. These pack-horse trains were common in the country down to the time of the Battle of Waterloo.

Ladies rode on horseback, generally on pillions behind their husbands or fathers, or some stout serving man. On the best lines of communication in England the ruts were deep, the quagmires abundant, and the descents precipitous, so the roads in Chapel-en-le-Frith parish may be imagined. Dr. Clegg, even in his daily rides, was in continual danger of being bogged in a swamp or precipitated into a stonepit.

As the trouble and cost of carriage were so great everyone lived as much as possible on home products. The country presented a very different aspect from what it does now. Wheat, barley, oats, and beans were grown where now nothing but universal grazing land is seen. The repeal of the Corn Laws and cheap ocean freights have made the growing of corn, except in the most favoured counties, unprofitable. It is a rare thing now to see a plough at work in the parish, whereas in Dr. Clegg's time six

* The Bagshawes of Ford are lineal descendants of one of the old foresters of fee, and their ancestors have held land in the parish for 600 years.

teams were sometimes at work on his farm; and he supplied his household with flour, malt, and meal, and his horses with oats and beans, from his own land.

Buxton, now one of the largest and most beautiful of our inland watering-places, which is situated only five miles south of Chapel-en-le-Frith, was in 1703 a mere hamlet, a Chapelry of the ancient Church at Bakewell. It had only a local celebrity, and the few visitors from a distance were lodged, as Macaulay describes, " in low rooms under bare rafters and regaled with oatcake and with a viand which the host called mutton, but which the guests suspected to be dog. A single good house stood near the spring."

The manners of the people were rude, sometimes brutal. A bear was kept at Sparrow Pit by a man named Shotter, which was brought into the town on fair days to be baited by dogs. Wakes, rush-bearings, and other festivities were scenes of drunken revelry and debauchery.

Not many events of historical interest have occurred at Chapel-en-le-Frith. In September 1648, part of the Scotch army which had been defeated by Cromwell at Preston, were brought prisoners to the town, about fifteen hundred in number, and were shut up in the Church. There they were kept for about a fortnight, during which time about forty died and were buried in the Churchyard, and ten more died on the first day's march, before they came into Cheshire. The Church bells were always rung in commemoration of the following events, viz. :—The Martyrdom of King Charles I., the 30th of January, the bells being muffled on one side and the ringing commencing on the evening before; for the Restoration, on the 29th of May, when it was also the ringers' duty to adorn the Church tower and porch with branches of oak; the birthday of King George III., the 4th of June; the 5th of November, and the evening before. They also ring the Old Year out and the New Year in; and Pancake bell still warns the busy housewife, on Shrove Tuesday, that it is eleven o'clock and time to begin the frying. At eight every evening, except Saturdays and Sundays, when it rings at seven o'clock, the curfew sounds over hill and dale, reminding us of our Norman vassalage, now happily so long gone by. The parish Clerk is responsible for tolling at these hours, and on him devolves by special custom the duty of ringing the " Sermon Bell " a few minutes before Divine service. This is the bell-tolling which, according to the strict letter of the law, the Officiating Minister should himself perform, but the ringers now receive an annual sum from the Incumbent for relieving the Clerk from this portion of his duties. The extra fees for ringing on public occasions were 6s. a day; but on the 29th May a further fee of 2s. was paid for placing the oak. On the 5th November the fee was 15s. and a goose at the Bull's Head Inn.

On Whit Monday there is a curious custom in this parish of providing every little child with a bottle, in which liquorice or

Spanish juice is put and then hung round its neck by a string. The children march to the wells and fill the bottles with water, which they then proceed to shake and suck at for the rest of the day. On this account that holy season is known amongst the juveniles as " Bottle day."

The congregation to which Dr. Clegg was called was formed in 1662, by the Rev. William Bagshawe, otherwise called the " Apostle of the Peak," after the Act of Uniformity had driven him, together with two thousand other conscientious men, from the livings that they held in the Church of England. Mr. Bagshawe was born at Litton, near Tideswell, on the 17th of January, 1627-8, and baptized the same month by Mr. Greaves, the Vicar of Tideswell. He was educated at Corpus Christi College, Cambridge, where he early showed a disposition for the Ministry. On leaving College he preached his first sermon at Wormhill. He was afterwards at Attercliffe, near Sheffield, for some time, where he lived in the house of Colonel, afterwards Sir John Bright. He was ordained at Chesterfield, January 1st, 1650-1. He was soon afterwards invited to Glossop, where he remained till St. Bartholomew's Day, 1662—" Black Bartholomew's Day," as it was called by the Dissenters. From Glossop he went to Ford, where he preached privately and in secret in his own house, and elsewhere.

The Declaration of Liberty of Conscience, in 1672, afforded a short relief to his persecuted flock, too short, alas ! so soon was the indulgence revoked. Despite existing prohibitions he continued to preach in " corners " and the people flocked to hear him like " Doves to a window." The Revolution brought happier times to the Nonconformists, and the little band of Presbyterians rallied with increased energy around their revered leader, and established a meeting house at Malcalf, near Ford, at which latter place Mr. Bagshawe resided, having inherited an estate there. Here they long worshipped in peace, drinking in the words of truth and holiness from the lips of the Apostle, those lips which were too soon to be closed for ever. " In the beginning of the year 1702," to quote from the Chapel Register, " the Rev. Mr. William Bagshawe, of Ford, departed this life. His last sermon was on March 22nd, 1701-2, from Rom. 8, 31. On Wednesday, April 1st, he lay in a slumber, towards night he called to have a hymn sung, and after a short prayer to which he added his Amen, he fell into a slumber, and seemed to breathe without difficulty, till on a sudden he gave a gasp or two and so quietly slept in Jesus. Having lived an eminently holy and useful life, he had the favour of an easy death. He was buried at Chapel-en-le-Frith and his funeral Sermon was preached by Mr. John Ashe, from Heb. 13, 7, and afterwards printed with his life and character."

Owing to the opposition of Mr. John Barber, who had succeeded his uncle as owner of Malcalf, and who had married a " high flown lady " with little sympathy for Nonconformists, it was decided to build a larger Chapel, within easier walking distance from Chapel-en-le-Frith; so land was purchased at Chinley and the present Chapel was erected in the year 1711, at a cost of £126 5s., almost all the money being given by members of the congregation. As may be judged by its cost, the building is a plain unpretending structure, very different to the modern Independent Chapels, glorying in spires, stained glass and organ chambers; but time has mellowed its aspect, so that its dark weather-beaten face, partly hidden in clustering ivy, forms no unpleasant object to the passer-by. The building of this Chapel so offended the zealous Churchmen of the parish that rotten eggs and stones used to greet the Dissenters on their way to worship, these assaults being mainly instigated by the unworthy Vicar of the parish, whose drunken, dissipated habits helped not a little the cause of Dissent.

Dr. Clegg does not seem to have been above the superstitions common at his time, as may be noticed from several entries in his Diary. The following curious letter was addressed by him to his friend Dr. Latham, who presided over the celebrated Dissenting Academy at Finderne, in Derbyshire, and who was the author of several controversial and other works. The Finderne Academy was one of considerable note, and many learned writers were pupils of Dr. Latham. Dr. Clegg's youngest son Benjamin was educated there. The following is the letter:—

" I know you are pleased with anything curious and uncommon in Nature and if what follows shall appear such, I can assure you from eye witnesses of the Truth of every particular. In a Church about 3 miles distance from us, the indecent Custom still prevails of burying the dead in the place set apart for the Devotions of the living: Yet the parish not being very populous, one would scarce imagine the Inhabitants of the grave could be strai'tned for want of room: yet it should seem so, for on the last of Aug'st, several Hundreds of Bodies rose out of the Grave in the open day in that Church, to the great astonishment and Terror of several spectators. They deserted the Coffins and arising out of the graves, immediately ascended directly towards Heaven, singing in Concert all along as they mounted thro' the Air; they had no winding sheets about them, yet did not appear quite naked, their Vesture seemed streaked with gold, interlaced with sable, skirted with white, yet thought to be exceeding light, by the agility of their motions, and the swiftness of their ascent; They left a most fragrant and delicious Odour behind them, but were quickly out of sight, and what is become of them or in what Distant Regions of this vast System they have since fixed their Residence, no Mortal can tell.

The Church is in Heafield, three miles from Chappell frith. 1745."

This extraordinary letter, which has given rise to considerable controversy, was published in " The Reliquary," 1860, by Mr. Llewellyn Jewitt, F.S.A., from a M.S. copy in his own possession. Its authenticity has been doubted; but granting its genuineness, may it not have been an illustration of the credulity of the people of Hayfield, and an example of the delusions which at times impose upon otherwise sensible people. This view was taken by the well-known novelist T. Adolphus Trollope, who writes "It seems to me, on carefully considering Dr. Clegg's letter, that he certainly did not mean to give his friend any idea that he (Clegg) believed that such an occurrence had taken place, but that he DID mean to tell him that such an assertion had been made at Hayfield. I fancy that he thought he was making a curious and valuable contribution to the history of the VALUE of TESTIMONY; and so he was if he would only have made his meaning a little clearer. If it can be shewn that a number of people at Hayfield did assert that they had seen such a phenomenon it would be—on the ground I have stated—a fact well worth having. And it would be an useful addition to the list of delusions indicating THE CONTAGIOUS nature of such. A fact of this kind could be paralleled and illustrated by sundry very similar stories; one of a ship's crew who ALL stated, on oath, that they saw the body of 'Old Booty,' a Wapping baker, much hated by them, thrown by the devil into the volcano Stromboli, then in eruption, as their ship passed it."—(T. Adolphus Trollope to W. H. G. Bagshawe, 1892.)

# AUTOBIOGRAPHY.

March 16th, 1729-30.

Being now through the mercy of God in the 50th year of my life and having passed through many changes, conversed with many persons, been concerned in many affairs, and had considerable experiences by which I either have or might have learned some wisdom, I have determined to leave behind me a short account of the most remarkable passages of my life, only for the private use of such of my children as may survive me, from which by ye Grace of God they may possibly learn to escape many errors that I have committed and avoid many evils that I have fallen into, and from the experience that I have had of a kind wise and watchful Providence all my life long, they may learn more entirely to rely on ye conduct of that Providence and to acknowledge God in all their ways; at least by this means I shall have an opportunity of recollecting, reviewing and lamenting many of my too numerous follies, faults and failings, and of calling to mind several very merciful appearances of God for me, and of his gracious dealings with me (which should never be forgotten) and of adoring His free rich and abundant goodness to a vile sinner.

I was born in a small village called Shawfield about two miles North West from Roachdale (a market town in Lancashire chiefly remarkable for the great quantities of White Bays and other cloaths made in that parish and sold there) on the 20th day of October, 1679, and baptized the Lord's Day following at the Parish Church by Mr. Jackson then Curate there, who had married my parents; he was also Chaplain to Mr. Holt of Castleton, and Master of the School when I learned there.

My father James Clegg is still living and a clothier in that village, as was also his father of the same name and his Grandfather. My Great Grandmother, Grandfather and Grandmother were all living when I was born and several years after, my mother Ann was the daughter of — Livesay of Berkle in the parish of Bury;[*] her father was a Zealous dissenter and had private Meetings in his house, when preachers of that persuasion were so bitterly persecuted in ye reign of Charles ye 2nd. I have heard her mention several ministers, amongst others Mr. Oliver Heywood and Mr. Naylor who used frequently to preach there. Her fathers brother was Minister at Chowbent, and afterwards conforming was Rector of Great Budworth in Cheshire; he married a Daughter of Mr. Cheetham of Turton whose father[*]

---

[*] Birtle is in the parish of Middleton.
[*] He was the uncle of the founder.

founded the Hospital and Library in Manchester. One of her Brothers was very loose in his youth and sold the Estate his father left him, and went into the army and became an officer, but what became of him I could never learn, but it was supposed he fell in ye Duke of Monmouth's Army in that rash invasion.

My mother was educated among the Dissenters and was always a Zealous one herselfe, a woman of great piety and still living.

My Grandfather had intended to educate his eldest son for the Ministry, who was a youth of eminent parts and piety, but he died a youth by a fall which caused a Penknife which he had about him to pierce his belly. His death was much lamented, especially by my Grandfather, whose hopes were thus blasted; for that reason as soon as he had the news of my birth he declared if it pleased God to spare me I should be educated for the Ministry, and in this resolution he continued so long as he lived.

1682. At about 3 years old I was visited with ye Smallpox which as I have been told was of so bad a kind as quite to deprive me of my sight for three weeks, and it was but narrowly that I escaped with life. About that time a Comet appeared many nights successively, and ye Great ffrost happened mentioned in our Almanacks, of which I have some dark confused remembrance.

Some children were taught to read in an house near us, and I often went to play there before my parents thought fitt to send me, but by hearing them learn, and playing with them, I shortly knew my letters and could spell before my Parents were acquainted with it, but then I was sent constantly and had scarce passed ye fourth year of my age before I could read very well.

When I went to School there my Great Grandmother died about 90 years old and not long after that my Grandmother departed this life.

1685. When about 6 years old I was sent to school to Mr. Joseph Whitworth a young Dissenting Minister at ffallinge about a mile from my father's house, who was not then allowed to preach, but was permitted to teach a good number of scholars for a time, and after an Indulgence was granted, he became assistant to Mr. Pendlebury and preached at Roachdale. Afterwards he removed to Cockey Chappell and was one of the Lecturers at Bolton: he was a good man but exceeding passionate and of a melancholy temper; he died some years ago.

1686. When about seven years old I was sent to the ffree school at Roachdale where Mr. Jackson always expressed a particular kindness to me, because he married my parents and Baptized me, and called me his son.

Whilst I was there I had some remarkable deliverances.
Following an horse one day at a considerable distance I found
an horse shoe; when I overtook the horse I observed he wanted
a shoe and began to doubt whether I ought not to deliver it
to the owner of the horse, but as I had not seen the horse cast
it, nor was sure it was his, I ventured to keep it in hopes of
selling it and purchasing some plumbs; which I did but with
an uneasy conscience. As I was eating the plumbs one of them
stuck in my throat, and went near to choak me, but at last I
parted with it when almost stifled. This made me reflect with
a sorrowful heart on ye dishonest part I had acted, and I resolved
to do ye like no more.

On another morning early as I went to School a large mastiff
which had broke loose from a Tannpitt near, met me with the
chain about his neck, I fled from him as fast as I could and
got to an house before he overtook me; but this made me ever
after unable to bear the sight of such a creature without fear.

On a Shrove Tuesday when ye young men of ye upper end
of ye school were shooting with bows and arrows at a cock, and
the rest of us made a lane for the arrowes to pass through, I put
my head a little too forward to see the shott, and an arrow shott
by a strong youth (Mr. George Brooks) struck me on ye left
temple and made a deep wound; it was at first thought to be
mortal, but being committed to ye care of a skilful surgeon it was
healed thro' the Mercy of God, but ye deep scar still remains.*

1687. In the Summer season I went to School daily on foot
two long miles, but when ye days shortnd I was boarded in ye
Town and only went home on Saturdays. I was first boarded
with Otwel Whitworth, a Linnen draper, usually called ye old
Presbyterian, a man very zealous that way: he prayed constantly
in the ffamily, which my ffather then did not, except on ye Lords
Days, and here they would be often talking to me about religion
but I had little sense of it, nor took much notice of their talk, being
much taken up with play amongst my companions, which were
none of the best; I often heard them swear and curse and was
sometimes inclined to do so too, but durst not venture, having
heard my Mother and others so often say it was a wicked practise.

Whilst I was here I was carried once or twice to a private
meeting in the night where old Mr. Pendlebury prayed and
preached; but I took little notice of anything said or done.

Whilst I was here I heard much talk of takeing off the Penal
laws and Test but did not understand much of ye meaning of it.

---

* Cock fighting, shooting at cocks with bows or stoning them were the
favourite diversions of Shrove Tuesday, a custom dating back in England
to the reign of Edward II. One old county ballad has the following lines:—
"And on Shrove Tuesday when the bell does ring
We will go out at hens and cocks to fling."

My landlord and his wife were earnest for their being taken off, and so were many others of yt way.

About that time there was much talk of the Prince of Orange, and Sir John Bland haveing drunk his health in Roachdale was clapt up in Prison by some of King James' Justices. The night following being a clear moonlight night I was engaged with other Boys in a mockfight. We had wooden swords and pistols, and were drawn up on each side the street, but on a sudden all our sport was spoiled by ye appearance of a troop or 2 of real soldiers upon the Bridge entering the Town with their swords drawn. We dispersed presently, and the soldiers marched to the house where Sir John was imprisoned, demanded him and carried him off. We heard after they were sent by the Lord Delamere to set him at liberty. Next morning all was quiet as if nothing had happened.

Shortly after ye old man I was boarded with died, and I was quartered awhile with one Andrew Bury, he was a ffudling man but his wife a serious christian. She would often be talking to me about religion, and one night as we sat by the fire I was asking some questions about the other world, and the punishment of wicked persons there; she told me they must be tormented in fire and that to eternity. I shall never forget how that word struck me. She left me in the house alone; I fell to thinking of that eternity, and the more I thought at it the more I was amazed, frightened, and troubled, I wept bitterly, fearing it would be my lott to be so tormented. Then I began to pray as well as I could, but continued full of trouble all that night, and for some time after, and I cannot say that impression ever quite went off. I then began to mind reading and sermons more, and remember I was much affected with a funeral sermon preached by Mr. Pendlebury when ye meeting place in yt Town was opened.

1689. About the year 1689 I was removed to a School at Oldham, about 4 miles from Roachdale, the master was Mr. James Lawton; he had been a Dissenting Minister in Derbyshire, but I know not that he was ever Ordained among them. I was boarded with John and Mary Whitacre who kept an Inn where several young Gentlemen and others were also boarded. Here I began to mind my learning more than I had done and came on pretty well. The Master was a melancholy man betimes, but fell to love strong drink too much. When he was with company at our Inn he would often call me to decline Verbs &c and answer questions before the Company, who applauded me and would often make me drink with them; and that turned to my disadvantage, for I was that way brought to relish and like it better than I ever had done before, but I had one companion in the house well inclined, viz Isaac Harpur son to ye Curate of Oldham. We often lay together and had sometimes some serious discourse about another world.

While I was at this School my Grandfather died very suddenly by a fall as he was endeavouring to climb over an hedge in his own ffields. He was a big corpulent man and advanced in years. His sudden death was a considerable loss to me, tho' I was not then sensible of it: he had a great kindness for me, and in all probability had he made a will, would have left me considerably, but what he had was divided betwixt my father and his sisters. He had all along been too much given to drinking, and alas had little space given him at last to repent. My ffather was exceedingly afflicted at his death and the manner of it, and for a time laid it much to heart, but ye impressions alas wore off too soon, and he continued too much addicted to the same practise.

Its one of the greatest disadvantages of Publick Schools, that the older Schollars very often set bad examples before the younger, and by filthy and lewd discourse and actions corrupt and debauch the tender minds of the younger. Some such loose and vicious youths were in this School and their talk and vicious practices had too much influence on me and others: for which reason I have often thought since, it concerns parents to take care what School they place yr children in, and what servants they entertain in their house, for the worst impressions made on me I received from conversing with some of both sorts that were lewd and wanton, the effects of which I shall have reason bitterly to lament as long as I live. And this has made me more unwilling to board out any of my children at any School at a distance.

1694. After I had spent about six years at Oldham School I was removed to Blakely, a private School was kept then by Mr. Jeremiah Barlow, a Dissenter, and many Dissenters in ye country about sent their sons thither, especially such as were designed for the Ministry. I was boarded at Edward Hides at Blakely Hall, and at first applied myself closely to my learning. I had begun to read Greek before I left Oldham and here took out of Leigh's Critica Sacra the signification and derivation of all the NOTED Greek words in ye New Testament and made some entrance on ye Hebrew. After some time I grew more remiss in my studies, being unhappily drawn aside by the cunning of a young woman in ye house, who had a design to procure me to marry her, and it was owing to a kind and remarkable Providence that it was prevented; ye Master of ye School discovered the intrigue, and informed my parents who hastened me away to the Academy sooner than otherwise I should have gone, and it proved a great loss to me that I had made no more progress in ye Hebrew tongue, before I was removed thence. I stayed not there much above a year, but have had reason to wish since I had never known ye house I was boarded at. The old man was a religious man but unhappy in his children.

1695. I was sent to the Reverend Mr. Franklands at Rathmel, a noted Academy in ye North. He had at that time about 80 young men Boarded with him and in ye Town near him, to whom he read Lectures with the help of an assistant. About a

dozen more came near that time, and were formed into a class.
Among others Mr. Harvey of Chester, Mr. Bassnet, and Murray
of that Town, Mr. Horrabin and others.   We entered with Logick;
I followed my studies very close and made as considerable a progress as most there.   One Tutor was a Ramist but we read ye
Logick both of Aristotle and of Ramus, and within the Compass
of the first year I was thought an acute disputant in that way.
But about yt time I fell into perplexing doubts about ye existence
of God, and a future state, which put me on reading all the books
I could compass on these subjects much more early than I otherwise should have done; but I went on with my studies thro'
metaphysicks and pneumatology which took up the three years I
spent there.   My bedfellow was Mr. Edw' Jolly a bulky young
man and not of the strictest morals, he was ye biggest man in ye
house and I the least.   But there were some serious youths, some
of our class and some seniors that met at our chamber for conference on some practical subject and prayer on the Saturday
afternoon, which was of great use to me.   On Thursday afternoon
we sometimes met for disputation, and often each night we had
a conference on what we had been reading that day.   About a
dozen of us agreed that one should sit up all night and call ye
rest up next morning about 4 o'clock, and we went to bed at ten
or eleven.   This we took by turns and spent about 14 hours each
day in hard study, during which time I eat very little and drunk
less, and found myself so very light and easy that I was ready
to imagine that with a very little help I could fly.   But my weak
constitution could not long bear this course.   The greatest incon-
venience I found was the coldness of the weather in yt climate
in the Winter, which affected my feet more than any other part,
and to this I thought it chiefly owing then in ye second year I
was seized with a swelling in my throat of a very great bigness.
The Surgeon called it a bastard Quinzey, there appeared a necessity for lancing it and my ffather was sent for to see the operation.
Ye Surgeon was very much afraid of meeting with ye Jugular
Arteries and did not pierce deep enough at first, but I bore it
well and beg'd he would go deeper, which he did and it succeeded
well and made a plentiful discharge of well digested matter, and
was soon healed and I had my health much better for some years
after it.

    After this illness I grew more remiss in my studies being
advized not to hazard my health, and to prevent ye return of a
like disorder I was persuaded to smoke Tobacco which drew me
into inconveinences, and caused the loss of much precious time.
Too much of it was also spent in conversing with the Ladies, Mr.
Frankland's daughters, which first led me to read Poetry and
Novels and such like trash, which I found reason to wish I had
never meddled with.   In the midst of these dangers I had the
happiness of a good wise affectionate real friend Mr. James Open-
shaw, a man of deep thought, of a clear head, strict morals, great
piety, and of a free communicative temper to me.   To his example
advice and instructions it was chiefly owing under God that I
was not quite ruined at that time.   I loved him entirely whilst he

lived and must ever honour his memory. He was born near Cockey Chappel in Lancashire, Educated at Blakely School, and when he left Mr. Frankland began to preach there-about, but after some time went with Mr. Harvey to Chester and assisted him. There he fell into a consumption which took him off, to the great loss of the Church of Christ.

1698. In the 3rd year that I spent at Rathmel, Mr. John Evans of Wrexham in Wales (afterwards Dr. Evans of Hand Alley, London) became my bed-fellow. He was a man of very good natural parts and Gentile behaviour, and a close Student. Mr. Jenkin Evans afterwards Minister at Oswestry was another of my familiar friends, a man of great seriousness. But there were others I conversed with sometimes of a different stamp by whom I was sometimes led into wild foolish ffrolicks, but blessed be God I was preserved in some good measure free from scandalous vices.

In this year I think it was that Mr. Thomas Davy a youth from the City of Leicester was unhappily drowned as he was bathing in the River Ribble. I heard a confused cry from the River side as I was reading in ye fields and hasted thither, stripped immediately and plunged into the River to search for him, being very well skilled in swimming and diving, but I could not find him. He continued in the water all night and was brought up by Hooks ye next morning. This made great impressions on me at that time; he was my Chamber-fellow.

1698. In October ffollowing the great and good old man Mr. Frankland died of ye Strangury, and a Universal decay. He read Lectures to us till the day before his death in his bed. I saw him depart; he committed us all affectionately to God and died in great peace. This was a wide breach; now we were left as sheep without a Shepherd. I was sent to desire Mr. Chorlton of Manchester to preach his ffuneral sermon which he did from Mat. 28. 20. . In that journey I was in great danger by the Rivers which were raised by the heavy rains. Mr. Chorlton was desired to take ye charge of ye Academy, but declined it. Afterwards others were proposed, as Mr. Lorimer, Mr. Tong &c but none was fully agreed on, and the young men began to drop away, some to one place and some to another, and so that Academy fell.

Mr. John Owen had been assistant to Mr. Frankland some time before his death and was I think with him then; a man of great piety a serious fervent preacher who was of great use to many, but his time was short, he did not long survive Mr. Frankland, but died in Wales. I think Mr. Chorlton after repented that he did not accept the call to Rathmel when he met with so much uneasiness in Manchester.

1699. When I left Rathmel I placed myself in Manchester for ye benefit of ye Library and ye conversation of other young Scholars yt lived there, and I boarded with Dr. Wild in Fennel

Street where Mr. Richard Miln of Mill Row near Roachdale also boarded. I had been very intimately acquainted with him at Rathmel and his conversation was of use to me at Manchester. But in a little time he was called to be Minister at Stockport, and I removed from Dr. Wilds to Mr. Chorlton. Several young men who had been under Mr. Franklands tuition at Rathmel also came about that time and placed themselves under Mr. Chorlton, who was admirably qualified for a Tutor as well as a Preacher. He read Lectures to us in the forenoon in Philosophy and Divinity and in the afternoon some of us read in ye Publick Library. It was there I first met with the works of Episcopius, Socinus, Crellius, &c. The writings of Socinus and his followers made little impression on me, only I could never after be entirely reconciled to the common doctrine of the Trinity, but then began to incline to that scheme which long after Dr. Clark espoused and published, but I admired the clear and strong reasoning of Episcopius, and after that could never well relish ye doctrines of rigid Calvinism. But all this time I continued too much addicted to levity and keeping company, and made not that good improvement of ye advantages I had that I ought to have done. Some acquaintance I fell into in yt Town that led me into evils that I have great reason to lament. But after I had spent little more than a year there I left the Town, and boarded with Jos. Dawson ye pious serious Dissenting Minister in Rochdale, and his good advice and pious conversation was of great use to me. There I began seriously and sadly to reflect on the foolish and sinful courses I had lived in, and resolved on another sort of life. I studied closely, read over most of the works of St Cyprian and many other Books, and there I first renewed my covenant in a solemn manner with God, first in private and afterwards at the Lords Table.

Whilst I boarded with him I began to preach, my first sermon was at Bispham in the ffildcountry of Lancashire on the Irish sea shore. The text was Rom : 14. 12. On ye Monday morning ye sea came over the Banks and over-flowed a great part of the country about, but soon returned and I got that night to Manchester but late. A little after I preached there again and took a tour to Leverpoole to see the Country. In that jorney I crossed ye River Ribble on horseback where it runs two miles broad and thought myselfe in Danger, but I had a good mare and a good guide and above all a Gracious God who carried me safe. After I had preached occasionally at several places for some short time my tutor Mr. Chorlton sent me again to Rathmel to preach to the small congregation there and officiate as Chaplain in the ffamily of my old tutor Mr. Frankland ; but there, having no Persons of Learning or ingenuity to converse with, I was by degrees drawn to converse too much with some gentlemen in the neighbourhood too much given to Tipling which was very prejudicial to me. Whilst I was there I visited York, Penrith and some other parts in the North, but made little improvement in my studies or preaching. A little before I left yt place Mrs. Mary ye second daughter of my old Tutor died of the Smallpox and ye youngest was married to a grocer in York.

By living too irregularly there and sometimes being wet and starved in carrying a gun and following my diversions, I contracted an ill habit of Body which appeared first in a Quinzey, then in a deep cough and weakness in my lungs which brought me into danger of a consumption. My father sent for me home, where I followed my studies at times, and preached occasionally at Ashworth and other places.

1701. That Summer I was obliged to attend my Mother to Knaresborough where I drunk first the Sulphur and then the Chalybeat waters, and made use of the cold Bath, and these greatly contributed to restore and establish my health. I spent some weeks there afterwards in company with Mrs. Chadwick, an intimate acquaintance, Mr. Billingsley of Hull, and other agreeable and useful companions. The rest of that winter I continued at home and part of ye next year. Whilst I was thus with my ffather the great and good King William died. I had ever thought him the greatest and best Prince that ever filled ye British Throne, and was accordingly affected with his death. I had then never taken the oaths to the Government nor any other oath. The abjuration oath was taken all over the nation when I was at Knaresborough, and when I came thence it was not known but that I had taken it there so I was never called on to do it; if I had, I believe I should have refused, because I was not satisfied that the pretender was not the son of King James, but upon better consideration I was convinced that the oath did not require me to swear any such thing."

Decr. 19th, 1708.　This day I resolved especially to be more diligent in my work as a minister and deal more freely and particularly with my hearers, as to which I have been too negligent proud and cowardly.

  (2)　I resolved against unsuitable company.

  (3)　Against unseasonable staying out of my house.

  (4)　Against excess and intemperance as to which my conscience reproves me.

Lord strengthen my resolutions and give me strength to perform.

Decr. 21st, 1708.　This day I preached a funerall sermon from Job. 19. 25. in which I fear I affected more elegance of speech than was suitable to ye capacities or wants of my hearers. My heart hath been harder and my performances more lifeless and cold then they were of late. Lord humble mee, help mee, give mee zeal, blow the fire!

Decr. 24th, 1709.　This day by ye goodness I and my dear wife had a great deliverance, an headstrong horse boggled and ran away with us in a very dangerous way and cast us off in a very dangerous place, yet neither of us received ye least harm. Adored be infinite goodness! What shall I render! I intend as a grateful acknowledgement of this favour to keep this day yearly as a day of thanksgiving to God and to give each year 5 shillings to ye poor on yt day.

March, 1709-10.　Strange heats and distractions occasioned by a very uncharitable and seditious sermon preached by Dr. Sacheverel for which he has been impeached and tryed; I never knew a wise nation thrown into such a ferment by such an empty blustering inconsiderable writer, but ye enmity agt Godliness is working in ye children of disobedience. Wee seem to be too ripe for a civile war now we have got a prospect of an end of a foreign one. May God prevent it! The rabble hath been up in ye City of Westminster, and demolished many meetings. Wee live in a poor but peacable part of ye Kingdom. Blessed be God!

Oct. 20th, 1710.　This is my birthday. I am now 31 years old.

Nov. 26th, 1710.　Yesterday the Parliament met. Great violence and sad disorders accompanied the Elections in many places. Ye Papists, Jacobites and secret enemies of ye present Government have been long projecting to get a Parliament of their Kidney. With this view Rehearsals and other Newspapers were writ and scattered to perplex ye consciences of ye people about ye succession to ye Crown, ye State Ministers Blackened, our successes abroad lessened, and mis-represented, our losses aggravated, passive obedience and hereditary right to ye Crown preached up. But all would not do, ye nation was easy at home in generall, and amazing success attended us abroad; proposalls were made for a peace, and it seemed to be near a conclusion to ye exclusion of ye pretender, and confusion of his friends. Upon this his party became desperate, and resolved to make one push for him before it was too late. So one Sacheverell, a proud daring blustering Clergyman of Oxford,was appointed to blow ye trumpet in St. Pauls in a sermon before ye Mayor of London : Ye Parliament impeached him of high crimes, &c., and charged him with condemning ye late revolution, &c. A mob was raised by his party to awe and affront ye Parliament; ye cry was against ye dissenters and ye heat ran through ye nation; all ye loose, debauched and disaffected people took Sacheverells part; addresses were sent up by that sort of persons out of many counties to have ye Parliament dissolved; ye Queen was terrified and so it was done, a new one chosen, and by bribery perjury and violence they have got a Majority in ye lower house. I think they will not sit long; if they do the nation will repent it.

I saw about Midsummer a strange Meteor a long and exceeding bright flame of fire, thick and obtuse before but small and bright behind come from ye North East, and flew very swiftly to ye North West casting a great light as it passed; it was seen in Scotland and all over the North. Oppositions in ye air are talked of, all which must be interpreted by future events. (1.)

1711. June 7th. After 6 or 7 very hot days with an Easterly wind, I observed in ye morning ye clouds arising out of ye East and West at the same time, but in ye afternoon ye Easterly wind abated and ye Westerly blew more strongly, and about two o'clock a large cloud arose out of ye West terribly black and gloomy, and wee heard a deep continuall rumbling thunder near half an hour together, followed by flashes of lightning, which was succeeded by violent gusts of wind and

(1). A High Church divine, Dr. Sacheverell, maintained the Doctrine of non-resistance in a sermon at St. Paul's with a boldness which deserved prosecution; and, in spite of the warning of Marlborough and of Somers, the Whig Ministers resolved on his impeachment. His trial in 1710 at once widened into a great party struggle, and the popular enthusiasm in Sacheverell's favour showed the gathering hatred of the Whigs and the war. The most eminent of the Tory Churchmen stood by his side at the bar, crowds escorted him to the Court and back again, whilst the streets rang with cries of "The Church and Dr. Sacheverell." A small Majority of the peers found him guilty, but the light sentence they inflicted was in effect an acquittal, and bonfires and illuminations over the whole country welcomed it as a Tory triumph.—(See Green's Hist. of the English People.)
Dr. Sacheverell was a cadet of the old family of Sacheverell of Morley in Co. Derby.

rushing whirlwinds, when the cloud broke with a prodigious noise and fell in one of ye most terrible tempests that was ever known in these parts, the stones that fell were many of them eight or nine inches about, and some larger; they were of a bluish colour and resembled pieces of solid ice, very irregular and extreme hard, these being driven by a violent wind accompanied by continuall flashes of fire from ye W.S.W. did abundance of damage to ye houses, corn, timber and mowing grass which was within the compass and course it took which was about 3 miles in breadth. It began about Macclesfield and came in a straight line from thence to . . . . Haugh, Heafield, and so (the middle of this entry is torn off) . . . . in the house shivered to pieces, ducks, geese, hares, pigeons &c were killed in multitudes, trees stripped of their bark, some torn up and others broke &c which afforded a dismal prospect after. Blessed be God my house suffered little, but some of my hearers had very great loss. This was a dreadful day and many thought ye dissolution of things was at hand.

1711. December 30th. At night between the hours of 12 and 2 in ye morning, the house of William Cooper in Chappell-en-le-Frith was burned by accident. He and a young girl (sister to Mr. Moult) lost their lives in the fire. I saw him after, and it was one of the most dismall spectacles I ever beheld. He had been too much addicted to swearing, lying and drunkeness, and his wife to covetousness and oppression by taking pawns &c. He had received ye Sacrament that day at ye Church. (2.)

Several persons besides have come to an untimely end in 2 or 3 weeks last past. A girl ye daughter of Wm. Rollinson was starved to death on Heafield Moor. Another woman starved near Edale End coming out of ye Woodlands, an old man at Hope, being struck down in ye fire by the breaking of a beam in his house, was burnt to death.

Febry. 20th, 1712-13. Many have lately been suddenly cut off. Three men and three horses were starved on Penistone Moor. One that kept a tavern in Sheffield and broke, ran about distracted and was found dead near Ughill. A boy was killed at Disley by a stoned horse, and a man drowned in a Colepit nr. Hockerly. May we be awakened to be ready!

Augst. 1st, 1714. Queen Anne died (ye same day ye Seizure Bill came in force) much lamented by some. The nation was, thought to be in very dangerous circumstances at that time, all ye great places of power and trust being in hands suspected to be inclined to ye Pretender, and if the ffrench King had been in a condition to have assisted him, the nation might have been involved in a long and bloody war, but by ye blessing of God

(2). "Sep. Wm. Cooper of this Towne and Hannah daughter of Thomas Moult of Tunstead, who was both burnt to death in their own house, he going as was thought to save the child's life but lost his own life Decr. 31st 1711."—Parish Registers, Chapel-en-le-Frith.

upon ye courage and vigilance of ye Lords Justices all was kept quiet, ye nation put into ye posture of defence and ye King George whom God preserve arrived safe. (Rest torn off.)

August, 1715. Lewis ye French King who had so long been a terrible scourge to these parts of Europe was called out of this world to give an account of his actions—very seasonably for these nations, ye disaffected here depending entirely on his assistance for setting a Popish Pretender on ye throne. Of late they have expressed their discontent in a most insolent and outrageous manner; mobbs have been raised in many parts of ye Nation to try ye affections of ye people and discover ye Pretenders friends, and ye mobbs in all places vented yr rage in demolishing ye meeting places of ye Dissenters without any manner of provocation. But ye Dissenters were known to be ye firmest friends to liberty and ye succession in ye Protestant line. Ye Meetings at Manchester, Shrewsbury, Stone, Newcastle, Moretown, Blakely, Greenacres, Burton, Bradwell, and many others were in a great measure ruined, and many others would have been if ye Parliament had not interposed by an Act to prevent such riots, &c. This was a prelude to the intended rebellion; for shortly after Providence brought to light a horrid conspiracy to destroy ye King and his family, to burn ye City, and raise people in severall parts of ye nation at once to restore ye Pretender and in Scotland Earl of Mar, lately Secretary of State to ye Queen, took up arms, and proclaimed James ye 3rd and 8th. He got together about 9 or 10,000 men and attempted to march into the Lowlands and go into England, but was met by ye Duke of Argyle and after a bloody battle forced to retreat; ye same day 1,500 Highlanders whom he had sent over ye Fforth being joynd by about 2000 English Lords gentlemen and were defeated and taken at Preston in Lancashire by ye Kings forces under General Wills with ye loss of about 130 killed and wounded; into this miserable distracted state hath party rage and blind-zeal brought these once happy and flourishing Nations: but our formality and looseness is ye grand procuring cause. Shall wee not see when the hand of ye Lord is lifted up, and His sword drawn.

Dec. 14th, 1715. Still this worthless provoking wretch is a living monument of divine patience. God hath brought me almost to ye end of another year, hath increased my family, hath continued my liberty, my health and strength, and provided comfortably for ye support of mee and mine.

Dec. 15th, 1716. The small pox hath been this year the Epidemicall disease, and very mortall about Manchester, Stockport, &c., but not so in these parts.

Oct. 20th, 1718. This is my birthday and when I look back on the time I have spent in this world (now 39 years) I am ashamed and in confusion to think I have done so little to answer the end of my creation, redemption and preservation.

Dec. 15th, 1718. This year is now drawing to an end, it becometh me to review and record the gracious dispensations of Divine providence both to ye Publick, and myself in particular. The year began with serious fears and rumours of designs to bring in ye Popish Pretender; Spain and Sweden visibly favoured him and entered into intrigues to support his interest. The Emperor was engaged in a dangerous war with ye Turks; ye King of Spain in imitation of his Grandfather broke through all treaties to lay hold on such an happy conjuncture to seize on ye Dominions of ye Empire in Italy; accordingly he invaded and seized Sardinia, Sicily, &c. To oppose and break these designs ye wise King George continued ye quadruple alliance engaging the principall powers of Europe to joyne in opposing any unjust attempts of any upon their neighbours, &c. In pursuance of this Sir George Byng (after the King had by his Mediation concluded a peace with ye Turks) was sent into ye Mediterranean to protect ye Emperors Dominions, where he destroyed a great number of ships of ye line, and took severall. War is proclaimed against Spain; ye King of Sweden is killed in Norway. A plott for destroying ye Regent in France and seizing ye Regency into ye hands of Spain comes on. Tis said Sweden had promised to invade Scotland from Norway. Ormond was to land forces in Ireland, while a French army was to invade England at once. Blessed be God! the snare is once more broken, the dissenters are eased of ye hardships brought on them in the latter end of Q. Anne's reign by the occasionall and seisure Bills, which Bills are now repealed after long and warm debates.

Sept., 1721. The latter end of this month this country was visited with the small pox. They broke out first in Kinder, where 2 young men sons of Fr. Gee were carried off by them. Shortly after John (B) his wife and one child died of that disease. A little after the family of John Froggat of Park Hall was visited and his eldest son John (a youth of great hopes) died, and about 30 others in and about Heafield; most of the families that were afflicted by them were broken. The small-pox were generally of ye confluent kind and more malignant than any I had ever seen before, accompanied by purple spots and nauseous smell (3).

---

(3). Small-pox was one of the greatest scourges in Europe during the 18th Century. It has been remarked by historians that at the end of the Century it was a rare thing to see any person unmarked by that disease. In 1694 Queen Mary of England died of the Small-pox, and in 1711-2 the Emperor of Germany, the dauphin and dauphiness of France and their son succumbed to the same disease. The Emperor of Russia, the Queen of Sweden, and Louis XV. were also its victims. Of the people millions perished both in Europe and America. In the middle of the Century two millions are said to have died in Russia alone. Whereas in London one in every fourteen deaths was attributable to small-pox, and in France the rate was one in ten. In Chapel-en-le-Frith it appears to have been endemic, and sometimes to have become epidemic. Children invariably took it as they now catch measles, and many middle-aged people died of the disease. Inoculation to prevent small-pox was introduced from Turkey by Lady Mary Wortley Montague. It was regarded at first with great suspicion, and was only tried on criminals condemned to death. The Bishops preached against it as an interference with the Divine Will; but two of the Royal family were inoculated in 1722, and Dr. Dimsdale of London gained his barony by successfully inoculating the Empress Catherine of Russia in 1768.

Jan. 9th, 1722. Our Physitians observe that an Epidemicall small-pox is generally a forerunner of ye PESTILENCE ; that dreadful scourge is now laying wast some parts of France, where a bloody Persecution raged some years ago ; may yt nation see the Rod, and who hath appointed it, and may we in this, who are so near them, and in such imminent danger of the infection see the Lords hand stretched out and learn righteousness.

Nov., 1722. Mr. Richardson, an Exciseman nr Buxton, a serious young man, was seized with ye small-pox. When I came to him I prescribed a vomit which succeeded well. Ye small-pox appeared on ye 4th day of ye confluent kind, and very malignant, with many purple spots, intermixed. On the 12th day ye 2nd feaver was very high and on ye following days he was delirious. I prescribed opiates and alexipharmicks and 2 episparick plaisters. Through Gods assistance he recovered.

Jan. 28th, 1722-3. I visited my parents and found yr family in health. In my return home I had a great and very remarkable deliverance. The snow had that day been melting off the hills, and tho' there had not been much rain the waters near us were raised considerably. It was late and almost dark when I came to ye ford below Bugsworth Hall, and my mare plunging hastily into ye deep water stumbled, and losing her feet was born down in ye stream. Thro' the Mercy of God I continued to sit her and with much struggling got her thro' the river. May I never forget that night ; t'was the 30th of January that I returned, and was thus mercifully preserved. May God have the Glory of it, and may I learn wisdom and reap Everlasting benefit from it.

May 2nd, 1725. The God of Mercy did grant His kind protection through my jorney and gave mee good success in the business I went about, viz building a place for worship and fixing a Minister at Buxton ; and blessed be His name that work goes forward. Considerable encouragement hath been given by pious Persons in London and other parts. God hath not been wanting to me. I witness for him, but I have (as I always have done) dealt very ungratefully and perfidiously with him since my return. I review it with shame. He is a long suffering God and I am a treacherous creature.

July 25th, 1725. The Chappel at Buxton is now finished through the good hand of our God upon us. Many sins and errors have been committed in ye management of it, for which

Vaccination was discovered, as is well known, by Dr. Jenner about 1780, and has proved one of the greatest blessings ever granted to the human race. Napoleon valued Dr. Jenner's services to mankind so highly that he liberated Dr. Wickham when a prisoner of war, at Dr. Jenner's request, and made a point of refusing him nothing that he asked for.

Some of the earliest subjects of inoculation probably in the Kingdom, and certainly the earliest in the parish of Chapel-en-le-Frith, were the children of Colonel Bagshawe, of Ford Hall, M.P., whose brother-in-law, Sir James Caldwell, of Castle Caldwell, Bart., was a very intimate friend of Lady Mary Wortley Montague.

I desire to take shame, but I hope in the main my aim and
intention hath been right. It hath cost me some pains in
travelling about 700 miles, and some moneys, but I believe I
shall be no loser. May precious souls be gainers by it. . . .
The place was opened ye 15th of July; Mr. J. Platts read ye
Scripture and prayed; Mr. Hardy preached from Ephes. 2, 20;
betwixt 4 and 500 were present; and on July 18th I preached
there in ye afternoon to a considerable number, from Col. 1, 2,
latter part. Laus Deo.

Sept. 10th, 1725. I was desired by my dear and good friend
Mrs. Eliz. Bagshaw to visit her 2nd son Adam, then dangerously
ill of ye small-pox in London. On ye Lords Day morning I set
out from Oaks with her daughter for London, lodged that night
at Nottingham, the next at Harborrow, the next at Wooburn,
and the next at London. Found ye young man very full of
small-pox of a bad kind, under the care of a London Physitian
called Knapp. Ye second feaver came on ye day after we came
there. Dr. Mead was then called in. Blisters were applied to
his arms, unseasonably as I thought, a strangury succeeded;
cordials were given but no sleeping potions were administered,
nor could I prevail to have them. The ffever continued to rise
much on Fryday; he had been without stool 12 or 13 days. I
urged the necessity of clysters, and many were administered, but
without effect. On Saturday a delirium and phrensy came on,
through ye violence of ye ffever, and on the Lords Day morning
about 4 o'clock he expired. This was a heavy stroke on ye
parents. We set out from London with ye body in an Hearse
on Wednesday ye 22nd, and came safe to Oaks on ye 26th, being
Lords Day. Laus Deo! (4.)

1726. (Some lines torn out). . . . . . Hottinger was
drowned in the Lake Leman with his 3 children. Some days
before this he found this verse writ on ye Doctor's chair when
he ascended it to read the lectures—
  " Carmina jam moriens canit exequialia cygnus."

Dec. 25th, 1726. I bound my son John apprentice to a
Quaker in Manchester thro' ye persuasion of some who I believe
meant well. My conscience was not easy when I did it. I
thought it was not well to place him where no ffamily worship
was likely to be performed, but I suffered myself to be overruled
by the advice of ffriends. Now the Quaker is broke, which is
likely to occasion much loss and a great disappointment. (5.)

----

(4). Mrs. Bagshaw was the only surviving child and heiress of Henry
Gill, of The Oaks, near Sheffield. This entry is a curious illustration of
medical practise in the last century.

(5). The Quakers were much disliked and despised by the Presbyterians
and other Nonconformists. In his Diary the Rev. Edw Burghah, the
Puritan Vicar of Acton in Cheshire during the Commonwealth, thus describes
them:—" 1655. The Quakers a giddy absurd sort of hereticks holding partly
with the Papists partly with the Anabaptists and partly with the Antinomians
began to start up amongst us, and this year multiplied in many places.
Their religion consists chiefly in censuring others, and railing at them

June, 1727. The great and good King George ye 1st departed this life at Osnaburg in Germany in ye same room in which he was born. His son King George ye 2nd succeeded peaceably to ye throne. Ye coronation of ye New King and Queen was ye most magnificent, and ye joy ye most universal that had been known.

In ye latter end of August or beginning of Septr many parts of ye nation were visited with a epidemicall ffever, in some parts of ye intermitting kind, and in others very malignant (remainder of entry torn off). This was succeeded by as Epidemical a disease amongst horses, but very few died of it.

Dec. 29th, 1727. This day visited a child at Bowden Head. Baptized a child at Gorsylow, after the parents Charles and Ann Shirt had professed repentance for ye sin of fornication they had committed, in ye presence of Christopher Bennet, and W. Carrington, and others.

(No date.) Today we had in ye prints a remarkable account of ye young Prince William's successful intercession for a poor persecuted Protestant family in France; and encouragement to hope for continuance of peace, by ye K. of Spain's compliance with our demands. Admirals declared E. of Torrington Admiral of the Fleet, Sir J. Jennings of ye White,
    Norris of ye Blue,
    Wager Vice-Admiral of ye White,
    Hobson of the Blue,
    Walton of the Red,
    Morris Rear-Admiral of the White,
    Hughes Rear-Admiral of the Blue.

Dec. 29th, 1727. The papers tell us the differences betwixt the K. of Spain and the K. of Great Brittain are accommodated.

Jan. 6th, 1727-8. An account of a terrible earthquake at Boston, New England, but little damage done. Ye news of the accommodation contradicted.

Jan. 13th, 1727-8. Little news of consequence. As yet uncertain if we shall have peace or war. Many losses at sea. Great complaints of deadness of trade, and many Robberies, especially in and about London.

Jan. 23rd, 1727-8. Ye Parliament met. God prosper yr counsels. Chose Arthur Onslow Esqre Speaker without opposition. Hopes of a peace increase.

---

especially Ministers, whom they despise and count as the dung of the earth, making it their common practice to disturb them in their sermons. They denied the Trinity, and denied the Scriptures to be the Word of God and said they had no sin. On June 9th two Quakers came into my Church with a lanthorn and candle while I was preaching: their design was (as they confessed) to have lighted a sheet of paper which they had as a sign of God's anger burning against us."

March 23rd, 1727-8. Agues and intermitting ffevers very frequent. Corn very dear. Meal at 13 and 14 pence the Peck and Malt at 36 shillings ye ——

Jan. 29th, 1727-8. At Macclesfield met Mr. Mills of Leek paid him 13£ 10sh rent for Mr. Degge. Spent 1s. 2d. Bought an almanack 6d. Promised to preach there the first Thursday in March, returned that night, called at Lydiat and on Mr. Byrom.

Febry. 1st, 1727-8. Chappell fair. Visited Mr. Byrom and Ann Gee at Lydiat. Paid for shoes 7s. 3d. Gave daughter Ann 6d, spent 7d.

June 3rd, 1728. That night I found a messenger from the Congregation in Newcastle in Staffordshire, to invite me to remove thither, by ye offer of about 60 pounds per annum. This is more by half yn I have here, but that is what I must not be governed by. Ye people here dont use me well, but I hope I am of some use especially to ye rising generation ; and God hath hitherto very comfortably provided for me. I have not the least reason to distrust him for ye future, and I am determined to spend ye remainder of my life where I think I can do him ye best service.

June 12th. Was at Wirksworth at a meeting of ye Derbyshire Ministers, Mr. Rogerson preached from Gal: 6, 8.

June 21. At Maxfield, lodged there at night.

June 22. Went on to Congleton in Cheshire and thence to Newcastle under Lime.

June 23. Preached there. "My Grace is sufficient." Had an earnest invitation thither in the evening from ye Heads of ye Society.

July 10th. Called to see Mr. Hatsel at Darton in Yorkshire ; passed by Lady Bower, Bradfield, Bolster stone, Silkstone, and Cawthorn ; Lodged at Darton with Mr. Mayo from Newcastle, found Mr. Hatsel distracted, thought to be occasioned by Cantharides given in his drink. Returned by ye same road home on the 11th very much fatigued with ye bad road.

July 17th. Returned home found Mr. Dawson of Roachdale and his daughters, Mr. Lawton, and cousin Mary Dawson and Mr. Venables at my house. Went with them to Eldon Hole and Castleton. (6.)

July 18th. Went to Chatsworth with them and returned.

July 27th. Got safe to Newcastle about one, and after visited Mr. Eaton at a little beyond it, who had spent many years in

(6). Eldon Hole is one of the Seven Wonders of the Peak, between Chapel-en-le-Frith and Castleton. It is not called after the Great Lord Chancellor—but the name is a corruption of Hell Dune—the place of Hell.

Egypt, Syria and Palestine, and brought back many rarities, medals, stones, plants and other curiosities.

Aug. 23rd. At home till the evening, then good old Mr. Finch, Minister in Norwich, sent for me and I enjoyed very pleasant and profitable converse with him till 9 at night; but he declines much, and I fear I shall see his face no more here.

Aug. 24th. At home reading and writing. This is Black Bartholomew Day, when so many of our pious and faithful predecessors were silenced in 1662. (7.)

August 25th. Preached twice on Gal. 6, 9. Catechized twice. Had two gentlemen with me in the evening, one from London, the other from Rye in Sussex.

August 28th. At home all day: had 20 reapers, the wind exceeding high occasions the loss of much corn.

Sept. 3rd. At the Meeting of Ministers at Knutsford, Mr. Wood of Chowbent preached from Matt. 5, 13, a serious sermon. Mr. Owen was moderator. Something done towards healing a breach betwixt Mr. Gardiner and Mr. Turner. (8.)

Oct. 11th. Met the Trustees and Heads of ye Congregation at Chinley Chappel, assured them of my purpose to continue with them. Parted in peace Blessed be God! may I be of more use than heretofore.

Oct. 19th, 1727. Twice at Chappel to meet Mr. Mills, who had sent for the whole years rent. A kind Providence had in ye foregoing weeks sent me in such supplies one way and another that I had a larger sum of money than usual by me, which made me expect I should have some extraordinary occasion for it; and now I find the reason. Such seasonable provision God hath often made for me. May I ever be thankful and learn to trust in him always.

Nov. 26th. At home hard at work till night, then went up with a letter. Received one from Mr. Calamy; had a promise of a degree from Edinburgh, but met with a disappointment.

Dec. 11th. An arbitration at Chappell. Mr. Ash was with me to give evidence about Mr. Barber's legacy. (9.)

(7). The 24th August, St. Bartholomew's Day, was celebrated as the day on which the Huguenots were massacred in Paris, A.D. 1572, and also as the day on which by the Act of Uniformity 2000 Clergymen were deprived of their livings in the Church of England in 1662.

(8). Sept. 11th to 22nd. The entries between these dates are written in Dog Latin, of which however the learned Doctor soon tires.

(9). The Rev. John Ashe, of Ashford, one of Dr. Clegg's greatest friends, and the author of many theological works, as well as a life of the Rev. William Bagshawe, named the Apostle of the Peak.

Dec. 19th. At Chappel with Mr. Kyrke, Mr. Waterhouse, Mr. Middleton, the last was extreme ill of the gout. The controversy about the disposal of Mr. Barber's legacy was unadvisedly referred to John Hall, Jo. Fletcher, Richard Turner, Rich. Dronfield and Edward Holgate the present Churchwardens and Overseers, who have quite deprived me of ye small share I formerly had of it, tho' they had sufficient evidence that it was all intended for the benefit of a dissenting Minister.

Jan. 16th, 1729. The water much out, durst not venture to ffernilee.

Febry. 9th. At night about 5 o'clock, the wind being very high, at W.S.W., with great rain, we saw many bright flashes of lightning, which were followed by some very loud and terrible claps of thunder. After the last, which seemed directly over our heads, the whole valley behind my house was filled with a sulphureous smoke. But I hear not of any damage sustained by any. Blessed be God!

March 12th. Set out for Derby, dined at Wirksworth, got safe to Derby.

March 13th. Preached at Derby from Matt. 18, 11. Many Ministers met and dined together. After preaching I visited Mrs. Morewood and Mr. Crompton and after that a young woman in the prison for ye supposed murther of a bastard: She seemed very humble and penitent. I spent about an hour in discourse and prayer.

March 17th. I was obliged to be at Chappell fair; sold two cows there. Several came for advice, and a merciful God sent in ye supplies I wanted.

April 8th. I was at Chappel to buy hay and to pay Easter dues.

April 14th. Set out with daughter Ann towards Roachdale; called to an old man at ye New Mill called Ralph Bowden, passed thence through Marple, dined at Stockport, visited Dr. Leach at Manchester, and lay with my son James in yt town.

April 15th. Came to Roachdale, spent some time with Mr. Pearson and other friends, and lodged with my aged parents at Shawfield. Found my mother very weak. .

April 16th. Had several infirm people with me, and visited some in that neighbourhood. Came again to Roachdale, and in the afternoon called upon Mr. Kay near Bury, and on Mr. Bradock in Bury. Saw Dr. Dixon and lodged at Bolton.

April 17th. Spent some time with Dr. Dixon, had his recommendation to Edinburgh for a degree.

April 23rd. Mr. Wood of Chowbent, Mr. Parr of Salford and Mr. Taylor of Manchester came to fish. I went with them down Edale, called at Joseph Hadfields; am to send a child there a Bible. Dined at Hope and lodged at Tideswal.

April 24th. Fished in the River Wye, returned to Tideswal, dined there and returned home. Not well satisfied to have spent so much precious time on diversions.

May 31st. At home all day; had a merciful deliverance, being violently thrown down by the horns of a madding cow, but had not much harm.

July 1st. Sett out for Roachdale with Mr. Scholefield. We met with 10 of our brethren at Stockport; Mr. Saml Eaton of Lostock was examined in order to his Ordination. I was chosen Moderator. He had forgot his notes, but gave us the substance of an excellent discourse on Rom 8th. After that he exhibited a Thesis de objecto fidei. Several objected, and many questions, chiefly relating to Scripture difficulties, were proposed and answered to satisfaction. I begun and ended the work with prayer, after which we had a cheerful dinner and some useful converse. We then went forward to Manchester and staid to see my son till it was late. We then went on to Roachdale, and lodged in an Inn there, our friends being all in bed.

July 30th. My mare was gone last night, and this day I cannot hear of her. I set out towards Martinside to seek her. She was found at Peazlowe. Blessed be God that I have her safe.

Aug. 6th. At Buxton with Mr. Arnold Kyrk, were kept too late by business. At night on our return my mare boggled and started aside near his house, and ran headlong with me thro' deep rutts and stonepitts, a considerable way before I could stop her. I was in very great danger but had no fall.

Sept. 1st. At home before noon. At noon set out for Knutsford. At Whaley Mr. Kelsal came to me; we refreshed ourselves at Pointon and came to Knutsford after Sunset. Found several of our brethren there.

Sept. 2nd. Mr. Saml. Eaton was Ordained there. Mr. Lea beginning with prayer, reading some portions of Scripture, and a psalm was sung. Mr. Mottershead prayed, Mr. Gardiner preached on John 16, 11. Mr. Eaton delivered the Confession of his Faith, Dr. Owen proposed the questions, Mr. Worthington of Dean Rowe prayed at ye laying on of hands, and I gave the exhortation and concluded.

Sept. 18th. This day is to be a race nr Bakewell and a prodigious number flock to it from all parts and notwithstanding ye general complaints of poverty can find money to venture on such occasions. (10.)

Sept. 30th. Stayed all day at Chesterfield and visited several good friends there, and had some pleasing conversation with them.

Oct. 5th. Preached at Chinley before noon from Heb. 12, 28, and afternoon at Buxton from Deut. 5, 29, to a considerable number. Stayed all night with Mr. Arnold Kyrke at Mr. Scholfields and bathed in the well yt night, and in the morning, for the pain in my hip, which was speedily eased.

Nov. 12th. I dined with my parents, spent some time with Mr. Dawson and friends in Roachdale, returned to Manchester in very heavy rain, where I met my son just returned from Blackburn, where he was married the day before. May God bless and prosper him and her. I lodged with my son in his room that night.

Nov. 19th. At home all day. We had a stormy night last night, and this day such a flood as hath not been known in many years. We hear it has taken down many bridges and drowned some cattle.

Nov. 23rd. On the 22nd at night I received my Diploma Medicum from Kings Colledge Aberdeen, with a kind letter from Principal Chalmers.

Nov. 26th. At home all day reading and writing. This night my son John came home from Manchester. He is afflicted with a severe cough and a quartan ague. He brings an account of a great mortality in that town, the ffever and small-pox being very mortal. Last week the bill of mortality in London amounted to nine hundred ninety and three.

Nov. 30th. I preached at Bolton both parts of the day from Eccles. 9, 10. The Pulpit and the day were so very dark that my notes were of no use to me. Blessed be God for his gracious assistance.

Dec. 2nd. I find the people of Bolton divided in opinion as to a Minister; many of them are unwilling to have one who practices physick, and many are uneasy that they have given up their right to chose one to 5 trustees. For these reasons it was not then thought proper to give me a call, and I am pleased that they did not. I find if I should remove thither this congregation would be in danger of breaking, and I should run a great hazard both as to health and ye comfort of life.

---

(10). Races used to be held regularly at Bakewell. "There were races about the year 1749 upon the Race ground on Bakewell Moor. Mr. Challoner's (of Blore) horse ran against a horse out of Yorkshire and a mare from Nottingham for a £50 plate which was won by the Nottingham mare."— Commonplace books of Mr. White Watson, F.L.S.

Dec. 18th. At home in ye forenoon. In ye afternoon was called to Armine Middleton. Found her distracted, I fear with hott liquors; ordered her a blister and some bolus, but with little hope of success, she being in a ffever of the spirits, and exceedingly puffed up of late.

Dec. 22nd. Sent my rent by Joh Wood. Ye Scotch cow was killed and proved to be very fatt.

Febry. 18th, 1729-30. This morning I lost a good cow newly calved and the calf is dead. Blessed be God yt the loss is no greater.

Febry 23. I accompanied Thomas Gee of Lydiat to Stanton to agree with Mr. Thornhill for the Deodand due on his fathers death. Returned by Ashford, called at Tideswell. I had heard some bad things reported concerning Mr. Kelsal's conduct and acquainted him plainly and freely with what I had heard. He confessed his folly in some things, and promised to be more watchful and diligent, and other things he denied. May God direct and assist him. (11.)

March 10th. Mr. White and his wife dined with me and I returned with them to Martinside where several of their relations were met and supped together. We stayed too late, and the night being very dark I narrowly escaped a dangerous fall into a stone pitt which my mare jumped into before I was aware of it. How many and how great deliverances have been granted to a sinful ungrateful creature; may I be sincerely thankful for this kind Providence. (12.)

March 17th. I went to Tideswell to hear what Mr. Kelsal had to offer in relation to ye scandalous reports spread of his behaviour. The day was rainy and cold, and I was much wet, but came away far less satisfied of his innocency then I hoped I should have been.

March 31st. I returned from Castleton with Will Swindells and went up to town with the Land Tax and Window Money, then I came home. (13.)

(11). A Deodand was a personal chattel which had been the immediate occasion of the death of any reasonable person and which was forfeited to the Crown to be applied to pious uses. But the right to Deodands had been granted out in most cases to Lords of Manors. Mr. Gee had been killed by being thrown off his horse, so the horse became a Deodand forfeitable to the Lord of the Manor.

(12). Martinside, near Chapel-en-le-Frith, was the residence of Mr. Arnold Kyrke, who was a friend of Dr. Clegg, and whose name occurs continually in his Diary.

(13). The Window Tax was first imposed in 1695 to defray the expense of and deficiency in the re-coinage of gold. It was retained by successive Ministers and gradually increased. It was abolished in 1851. This was the most abominable Tax ever imposed upon the public. Its evil effects are still visible in most of the houses in the Peak, where infrequent windows cause dark and ill-ventilated houses.

April 13th. At home in the afternoon with plowers and harrower. A very fine day.

April 15th. At home gardening in the forenoon. In the afternoon I went with Mr. Arnold Kyrk to Buxton where I had desired some of that Congregation to meet me to consult about Mr. Scholfields stay or removal. I found them so very indifferent that not one of them would subscribe or promise to contribute one penny for his continuance amongst them.

April 17th. At home all day, working in the fields and ye garden, and reading and writing by turns. This day I received a box from London and in it Mr. Wright's book called " Ye great Concern," &c.

April 29th. I went with my wife to Martinside and dined there. Mr. Scholfield came thither to take his leave. He leaves Buxton unwillingly, but the unkindness of that people forced him away.

May 5th. (At Chesterfield.) We went out to take a view of The Earle of Scarsdales seat called Sutton. Its a noble seat and a fine situation; the furniture is rich and new, and the gardens well kept, but want water. (14.)

May 6th. I sett out for Offerton and dined there with my sister Ruth and her husband whom I had not seen before, thence I went to Derby and lodged at the " George." (15.)

1730, May 7th. I visited Mr. Rogerson and Mr. Shawe; from the former I recd ye collection for the Peak and Lady Armine's bequest. I preached there from Acts 20, 24 ; about 15 Ministers were present. We dined together at ye " George." After dinner I set out for Calah again.

May 17th. Catechized about 30 children ; many little ones are now ill of ye measles, my youngest son has had a bad time of them, but blessed be God is now recovering.

May 29th. Mrs. Cresswell of Tideswell called on me to go with her to Disley to meet Mr. Parr of Salford to procure Tuition

(14). Sutton Hall, at Sutton-in-the-Dale, near Chesterfield, was built by Nicholas 4th and last Earl of Scarsdale, who died in 1736. It was purchased after his death by Godfrey Clarke, and through the Clarkes it came into the possession of the Marchioness of Ormonde. It is said that the old peer with a coronet on his crutch in one of Hogarth's Marriage a la Mode Series is a caricature of the last E. of Scarsdale, who was very vain of his title and the symbols attached to it.

(15). The " George " at Derby was in former times an inn of considerable note, and was situated at the back of Sadlergate and Irongate, where the name is still retained as the " George Yard." The inn was in appearance worthy the " Tabard " and other old hostels of Southwark, and was galleried on the sides of the yard.

of her daughter an Idiot; a plott having been laid to steal her away. We dined at Disley and returned in heavy rain. (16.)

June 7th. I preached twice and administered the Lords Supper to near a hundred communicants, and Catechized near 40 children in ye afternoon, but was much fatigued. I find I cannot go on long at this rate.

June 11th. I was called to Chappel to assist a poor widow at ye Copy-hold Court.

June 24th. I set out with John Bennet for ye Oaks and dined there. Bowled awhile on the Green.

June 25th. We had the double lecture at Chesterfield. I preached from I Sam 3, 18. About 18 ministers present. Dined at ye inn, but the gentlemen in ye town bore ye expense. Mr. Kelsal's case was considered. He owned himself guilty of many irregularities and indecent liberties, but denied the grossly criminal facts he was charged with by fame, and was admonished and suspended for 3 months.

June 27th. Mr. Gellebrand a young Minister from Lancashire came and lodged with us.

July 14th. I went to Buxton to meet Mrs. Adcroft and some Manchester friends, and thence with them to Tideswell, where I dined, and settled some matters with Mr. Eccles and Mrs. Cresswell relating to ye Commision of Enquiry as to her daughter Alice's Idiocy.

July 16th. The Commission was opened at Town Head, Mr. Cheetham Mr. Parr and I were Commissioners (in Lunacy). The Jury were sworn, witnesses examined, and Alice Hill was found and presented an Idiot. This was done to prevent her being stolen away and ruined by a worthless fellow who had attempted it, and to secure her Estate for her use while she lives and for her right heirs after. Many censures pass on this proceeding, but knowing my intention in it to be just and right I have no reason to regard 'em.

July 24th. Visited several sick persons about me, and was very busy amongst my haymakers. We got a good deal into ye barn very good. At night I went up to Chappel to seek for mowers.

Sept 14th. I attended my father-in-law to Edale to visit my mother much indisposed. She was seized whilst I was there with a most violent Hysteric fitt exactly at the time ye moon came to the full.

---

(16). Tutors and guardians were appointed to look after the persons and property of idiots.

Sept. 19th. On the 18th at night the wife of John Armstrong told me the night her child was seized with the small-pox, her husband being in bed with her and the child, both she and he heard a noise as if some one had walked sharply over the chamber and gone under the bed. The husband got up and searched the room but found nothing. The child lay betwixt them but would needs be removed to ye side next ye wall, but presently cryed out " Ye Boggard has touched me," and would lie betwixt them again. A night or two before, ye wife being in ye house, herself heard a dismal noise like ye cry of a child, ending in a mournful tone. Ye like walking she heard again in ye chamber ye week but one after, when her sisters child was seized. They were both seized with ye most violent and deadly infection I had ever seen. (17.)

Sept. 28th. I set out with Mr. Tricket to see some remarkables in several parts of ye Peak. Called at Money Ash ; went by Middleton nr Youlgreave ; came to Winster about noon. Saw 3 curious Engines at work there, which by ye force of fire heating water to vapour, a prodigious weight of water was raised from a very great depth and a vast quantity of lead oar laid dry. The hott vapour ascends from an iron pan close covered, through a brass cylinder fixed to the top, and by its expanding force raises one end of the Engine, which is brought down again by the sudden introduction of a dash of cold water, into ye same cylinder which condenseth the vapour. Thus the hott vapour and cold water act by turns and give ye clearest demonstration of ye mighty elastic force of air. Thence we set out for Wirksworth, visited Mr. Hankinson ye minister there, who is in danger of going into a Pthisis Pulmonalis. Thence we went to Matlock Bath. The situation is charming and ye water very like that at Bristol, and must be exceeding beneficial in many cases. Two good houses are built for entertainment, but the Bath is not nearly so warm as Buxton. (18.)

Sept. 29th. I ascended the hill above Matlock and had a surprizing view of ye Country round. Then went into ye bath, and after that walked about ye river banks till near noon. Then Mr. Hankinson came to me and my friend Mrs. White from Calah. We dined together and soon after I set out with Mr.

(17). Boggarts were a sort of household ghosts much believed in and feared by children in Lancashire and Derbyshire. This Evil Spirit of the place was a kind of household policeman, and children were terrified into good behaviour by the threat "The Boggart el tak thee."

(18). The Seven Wonders of the Peak were Chatsworth, The Peak Cavern, Mam Tor, Eldon Hole, The Ebbing and Flowing Well, Buxton Well, and Poole's Hole. The celebrated Thomas Hobbes, of Malmesbury, who was a frequent visitor at Chatsworth, wrote an Epic poem in Latin called " De Mirabilibus Pecci, being the Wonders of the Peak in Derbyshire," dedicated " Ad nobilissimum Dominum Gulielmum Comitem Devoniæ," etc.
Steam Engines were at the time of Dr. Clegg's visit to Winster in their infancy, for although the Marquess of Worcester, in 1663, invented a machine "to drive up water by fire," no practical engines were manufactured until Watts' invention, in 1765.

Hankinson to view Middleton Bath nr Bonsal and returned by Cromford to Wirksworth. I made some tryals of two springs there, one a stinking sulphur near akin in qualities to yt at Knaresborough; the other is a strong Chalybeate.

Oct. 2nd. This morning I begun to use ye flesh brush and design to continue it.

Dec. 14th. At home all day reading an account of Persia and ye countries about it.

Dec. 17th. Heard that an execution was served on George Thornhills goods, sent for a cow he had of mine in haste and got her. This wretched condition his unclean life and continued intemperance hath brought him and his numerous family into.

Dec. 19th. Workmen came to fell a tree; as I stood by them I narrowly escaped ye loss of an eye. Blessed be God!

Jan. 1st, 1731. Sometime spent in praise and prayer. At night I looked over ye accounts of ye year past, and found ye expenses to amount to 120 pounds. So plentifully hath God provided for us.

Feb. 27th. I was at home all day preparing sermons, which work I find goes much harder with me now than formerly, but I dare not neglect it. I cannot satisfie myself in preaching old sermons unless in a case of extreme necessity, and when I do so I find it neither so good for myself nor others.

March 5th. My wife set out for the funeral of John Vernon, a youth educated among ye dissenters, but removing into ye Peak fforest he left us, and afterwards was married to Dorothy Lomax, widow to J. Vernon, a woman twice as old as himself. His health began to decay soon after and he died of consumption. I was never called to him and am glad I was not.

May 9th. In the evening Mrs. Waterhouse and her daughter White called on us. Mrs. White was ill and at first we suspected a fitt of ye gravel, but too soon it appeared they were ye pains of Travail. She was very ill some hours, a midwife was called and she was delivered of a small child about 3 months growth; and next morning of a mole or false conception. T'was well she called, for she could not have got home. I believe this miscarriage was owing to a fright at Chesterfield as she came, where the man that went for her was struck by a stoned horse and taken up for dead; since that she has almost always been ill and often full of pain.

May 14th. Mr. White gave me two guineas for advice and attendance on his wife. Thus Providence sends us in supplies.

June 6th.  Preached twice.  Made a collection for ye repair of ye Church at Chappel-en-le-Frith which amounted to twenty shillings.

August 10th.  I set out with my wife, and Mrs. Mary Kyrke for Chesterfield.  Called on Mrs. Jackson at Ashford; her maid had a little before got a fall and broke the radius in ye arm.  I assisted ye surgeon to reduce and sett it.  We dined there and they set out with us for Chatsworth.  Before we got there the axis of her chaise broke, so we left them at Edensor, and I accompanied my wife and Mrs. Kyrke to Chesterfield, and came there about eight at night.  Several ministers were come, and I spent the rest of the evening with them, concerting the method of the next day's work when Mr. John Holland was to be Ordained.

August 11th.  Spent sometime and breakfasted with Mr. J. Mills.  Then the Ministers met at Mr. Smalleys and heard Mr. Holland's confession in private. Thence we went to ye meeting-house.  Mr. Smalley began with prayer, reading ye Scriptures, and a Psalm.  Mr. Waddsworth of Sheffield prayed before sermon. I preached from Matt. 1, 18, and gave out a Psalm.  Mr. Platts took ye confession and proposed ye questions.  Mr. Pigot prayed at ye imposition of hands and Mr. Ash gave ye charge and concluded with prayer.  The whole work was carried on with seriousness and decency and to ye satisfaction I hope of all present. Ye Ministers dined together and the evening was spent at Mr. Will. Mills' with many friends.

Augst. 17th.  Had more reapers and spent ye forenoon with them.  I found a messenger to call me to good old Mr. Bateman of Hartington.

Augst. 18th.  I set out with ye servant about 2 in ye night, came to Hartington before six, found the old gentleman dangerously ill of a diarrhœa and violent vomiting, prescribed to him, and he was relieved as to those disorders but his strength was so spent before I came, and his age so far advanced (being 82). that I had no hopes of his recovery.  I lodged there that night.

August 25th.  We began to lead corn, and I worked at it hard till noon.

August 27th.  An horrid and barbarous murder was committed near Dane Bridge, in the road between Macclesfield and Leek some time ago; one Nadin murdered Mr. Buck a grazier, at the instigation of Buck's wife it is supposed, with whom he had lived in adultery.  And now the said Nadin is condemned, and to be gibbeted.

August 31st.  I had promised to visit Madam Jackson at Ashford.  My way thither (from Macclesfield) lay nr Leek, and this being ye day appointed for ye execution of Nadin, Mr. Culcheth and Mr. Eaton &c. went along with me that way. He was

brought to Leek the night before; we meet him on the common
the gibbet was erected on. The Sheriff Mr. Drakeford, whom I
knew, came first with his men, then ye Clergyman yt had assisted
ye criminal, then the man who carried the Irons he was to hang
in; then came the prisoner, then the gaoler and last ye Hangman.
Ye Curate of Leek spent an hour in praying with and exhorting
him; then the 51st Psalm was sung, and after some time ye
executioner did his office. I went home and dined with Mr. Mills,
and spent some time with him and the Sheriff, then set out for
Ashford and lodged there. (19.)

Sept. 7th. At home most of the day, overseeing ye reaping
and leading of my wheat.

Sept. 14th. I was invited to Park Hall and dined there with
the Vicar of Glossop and his wife. My wife was with me and
we returned well pleased with our entertainment and cheerful
company.

Sept. 15th. I was up pretty early and went out to meet
Mr. Bagshaw and other friends at Small Dale to course hares.
Several gentlemen were with us, and had what they called good
diversion, but to me its far from being as diverting as formerly.

Sept. 24th. Close at work transcribing for ye Press, and
got that work finished at night.

Oct. 7th. I spent the forenoon with my brother in shooting.

Oct. 9th. Sent my man to Manchester for 4 Scotch cows.

1731-2, Jan. 3rd. I dined at fford and went after with
sister Rachel to Castleton. Visited many children in ye small-
pox, about 20 have died there of that disease and about 60 are ill.

1732, May 16th. Set out for Stockport to assist Mrs. Milne
in valuing her late husband's books. He died May 5th, 1732,
after a long indisposition. He was a friend I valued, having lived
in an intimate acquaintance with him near 40 years. He had
a numerous library. I got to Stockport before noon and fell to
work till night, Mr. Hardy and Mr. Jones assisting me. I
lodged at Mrs. Milne's.

May 17th. I continued still valuing the books from six in
the morning till ten at night and was very much fatigued. Lodged
there.

May 18th. I continued valuing the books till ten before noon,
when we finished, having gone through 1500 books and many
of them books of value.

(19). Hanging in chains was at that time a common form of punishment.
Gibbets with fragments of rusty chains swinging in the wind and terrifying
the belated way-farer were not uncommon in the High Peak fifty years ago.
Hanging in chains was abolished by Act of Parliament in 1834.

May 30th. At Manchester. Was with Mr. Isaac Clegg at breakfast. Mr. Butterworth, Mr. Walker, Mr. Winder, and Mr. Mottershead there. The subject of our conversation was ye most proper method for procuring the Repeal of the Test Act, &c.

June 7th. Last night Brother Jo. Clegg came to us and brought with him an Irish gentleman who is absconding from an enemy, who prosecutes him not for a crime, but on account of an unfortunate bargain. My brother desires me to let him stay a while in my house till he can by his agents come to an agreement with his adversary.

July 28th. I was at home all day, but much indisposed with a cold. I diverted myself with turning with the Lath, and such odd work.

August 7th. I set out with Mr. Clements and his son to see Chatsworth. Called at Tideswell and visited some sick, and called again on our return. Prayed with Sarah Shirt and called on Mrs. Cresswell, but stayed not long. In our return through ye fforest my young mare fell with me and cast me over her head. My head happened to pitch on ye side of a causeway, and I was so stunned with the fall as to be taken up for dead, but thro' the mercy of God recovered and came home after. My face was hurt and my cheek cutt and I have had great pain in my head since. Blessed be God for this deliverance.

August 18th. At home all day. Began to reap ye wheat. One ffurness came to me to desire my assistance in recovering a daughter lately perverted to the Romish religion, which I readily promised, leaving it to them to appoint the time and place.

Aug. 21st. At home most of ye day reading some Treatises against ye Romanists.

August 22nd. Set out for Lees to meet Mr. Stringfellow and made some proposals for a match between Mr. Carrington and his daughter.

Sept. 6th. I set out for Ashworth, dined with Justice Hallowes, and returned that night to Manchester. The horse races began that day, but I got to Manchester before they were over and came not near them.

Oct. 10th. At home before noon: After set out for Tideswell to assist Mrs. Hall in a Commission for Examining witnesses in a suit betwixt her brother and her. Ye Commission was finished yt night, and I lodged at Mr. Hadfields, but was kept up late.

Oct. 13th. Baptized a child of William Grant of Chinley called Michael, he and his wife confessing their sin and professing their repentance before a considerable number of ye congregation then present.

Oct. 19th. At home in the forenoon. In ye afternoon went up to town, had a horse rider to break my young horse, am in hopes he will do well.

Nov. 12th. At night my son James came to us; he had been pursuing a servant maid that overran him. He found her at Hope and in his passion treated her ill, for which he was likely to come into trouble and deserved it.

Nov. 21st. I met an emissary of ye Church of Rome at Sheffield. Some of that persuasion had seduced the daughter of Luke ffurness to that persuasion, and at ye request of the father I promised to meet any of that party and debate ye matters in controversy before ye daughter and other witnesses. The debate lasted near five hours; about 20 were present. Most of the company were fully satisfied, but ye young woman seemed obstinate after all. I had many fears about this dispute, lest a good cause should suffer through bad management on my side, but God assisted me, and I had reason to be thankful.

Dec. 14th. At home before noon. After dinner I spent some time with Mr. Bagshaw and Mr. Waterhouse at Chappel. Had a letter from Mr. Wadsworth about ye proceedings of the Dissenters in relation to the repeal of ye Corporation and Test Acts. I fear they are too forward in pushing that matter so warmly.

Dec. 26th. Preached at Whitehough Head from John 8, 56, and some time was spent in prayer. After that rid over to Chappel where was a Parish Meeting about the Bells. (20.)

1732-3. Jan. 5th. Was at home all day. Had several of my young friends and neighbours at supper at night and several stayed all night.

Jan. 31st. At home all day. Mr. Waterhouse, Mr. Batty and brother Champion dined with me. The co-heiresses of Fras.

---

(20). "1741. The great bell in our steple was taken down to be cast upon Friday 27th June, and as it was coming down the pulleys broke, and the bell fell to the ground, and brought all before it. The man who was above to guide it was one Ezekiel Shuttleworth a joyner in this towne, he seeing the pulleys break could no ways help himself but came after it, a ladder with himself, and a little crow of iron in his hand; and yet by God's great preservation had little or no harm. The great bell was recast at Wigan 6th Aug. 1701, by Mr. William Scott who was Alderman of Wigan the same year."—Parish Register, Chapel-en-le-Frith.

There is a peal of six bells in the tower. They are inscribed as follows:—
1. "Peace and good neighbourhood," followed by initials A.R., between which is the figure of a bell. This is the mark of Abraham Rudhall.
2. "Prosperity to this Parish" and same mark.
3. "We were all cast at Gloucester by A. Rudhall, 1733."
4. No inscription.
5. "Jasper Frith and John Wainwright Churchwardens. 1733."
6. "I to the Church the living call, and to the grave do summon all. 1733."

The Rudhalls had a celebrated bell foundry at Gloucester from the end of the 17th century till about the year 1830.

Gee were examined in order for a fine to enable them to sell ye Estate in Chinley, and ye examination sent up by ye London carrier. (21.)

Febry. 6th. I set out with daughter Ann for Manchester, dined at Stockport, and lodged with Son James, found him and son John ill of ye common distemper. This week ye bill of Mortality in London amounted to near 1600. May it please God to stay this!

Febry. 10th. Ye bill of Mortality in London last week amounted to 1585.

1733. April 26th. This morning my dear daughter Ann was married to Samuel Waterhouse. May the blessing of God be on them and make them blessings to each other and to all that are about them.

April 27th. At home most part of the day, reading Mr. Neals Hist: of the Puritans.

May 8th. I had a call to Mrs. Jackson of Gainsborough. Came to Chesterfield and lodged at Mr. Slaters.

May 9th. Set out with Mr. Slater, Mr. Ashe &c. We dined at Worksop and came safe, thro' ye mercy of God, to Mrs. Jackson's about 6.

May 10th. I considered Mrs. Jackson's case and consulted with Dr. Huntington, who had been concerned for her, and saw ye apothecary and lodged at her house again.

May 14th. I rid over to Widow Gee's in Chinley and prayed with her daughter Ann. Dined at John Carringtons, went thence to Heafield, bought some timber, and called at Jos. Ashtons in my return. I found his wife going fast towards the grave; her days must be few.

May 15th. I was much indisposed all morning in my stomach and especially after dinner. For which reason I rid over to Buxton and bathed in ye well, and drank several glasses of St. Anne's Well and returned much better.

May 23rd. I rid over to Heafield to bring some timber thence into Chinley for repairs. Called and sat awhile at Henry Kyrke's with the Vicar of Glossop and some others.

June 1st. I was at home all day, but neglected my work too much, and mispent too much time in making an arbour &c., which occasioned me to be too much in a hurry afterwards.

(21). A Fine was a fictitious suit, by which cumbrous method estates were transferred. They were abolished by the Fines and Recoveries Act, 3 and 4 Will. 4.

June 10th. I preached twice. Expounded in the morning and Catechized twice as usual. Much spent, but far more afflicted at night when son James came from Manchester and brought with him my son Joseph, whom his master has turned out on account of his intemperance and injustice to him. This filled our poor family with unspeakable grief. We have reason to look on it as ye greatest affliction that ever came upon us.

July 3rd. I set out to accompany Mrs. Cresswell to Doncaster to meet Dr. Johnson from London. I dined at Tideswell, we called again at Sheffield and lodged at Rotherham.

July 4th. Set out early for Doncaster and was there about ten in the morning, Dr. Johnson came about noon. We dined with him and had his company till about 5. Then he set out for ye North and we for Sheffield, where we lodged.

July 5th. I visited Mr. Wadsworth and dispatched some other business. We dined at Small Dale and stayed some time diverting ourselves till ye cool evening came on, and I came home about 10.

July 30th. My daughter came over from Heafield about a troublesome business she had brought herself into by an indiscretion. I carried her towards home and returned thro' Chinley.

July 31st. I attended the funeral of Robt. Carrington son of James Carrington of Chinley House. He had left ye Dissenters and married unhappily. His time after was very short and full of trouble.

Augst. 29th. I set out for Macclesfield with James Carrington Junior and Christr. Bennet to enquire into the cause of Robt. Carringtons death. There are violent suspicions and gloomy presumpteons that his wife destroyed him by giving him Cantharides; but we could not find sufficient positive proof. I returned that night in heavy rain.

Sept. 5th. I sent for daughter Ann, but she was prevented by a misfortune; an horse she had borrowed was hurt. I went to Heafield to agree the matter; it must be much to their loss. May God sanctifie it to them!

Sept. 21st. At Wirksworth. Visited Mr. Turner, Mrs. Bockin and Mr. Mather, then set out for home in company of Mrs. Harrison, a widow from Warrington. We dined at Tideswell and came safe to my house in good time and found all well. In this journey I hear of T. Cresswell's marriage. I fear that youth is quite undone.

Oct. 22nd. After dinner I carried my wife to Lydiat and visited a young woman at Bradshaw Hall seized with Hysterick fitts threatening a palsy.

Oct. 31st. This morning I had information from a friend that ye Churchwardens of Chappel-en-le-Ffrith have taken out a citation for my appearance in their Court to answer for non-payment of ye Church assessments; upon which I went up to Chappel-en-le-Frith and in the house of John Wainwright one of ye Churchwardens I made a tender of three pounds and thirteen shillings for the said assessments, about eight o'clock in the morning, in the presence of Mary Wainwright, Mother of ye Churchwarden, and George Wright of Chappel, Skinner.

Nov. 1st. This morning I was served with the citation or process; altho' I had never refused to pay these assessments, and the Churchwarden had my money in his house at the same time. In the afternoon I went up to Chappel on business. (22.)

Nov. 18th. Preached twice from Colos. 4, 3, 4, to a full congregation. A collection was made for the Church Clock in the evening of about 12 shillings.

Nov. 22nd. In the afternoon I went up with my wife to Chappel and made a tender again of my Church Levies to J. Wainwright, at ye sign of the Roebuck, in the presence of Joshua Wood, Peter Wood and Ralph Kinder of Heafield, but he refused to take the money.

Nov. 26th. At home in the forenoon reading Dr. Short's account of Mineral waters, &c.

1733-4, Janry. 11th. Thus within the space of 19 days I have been called to preach 17 sermons, and I humbly own the goodness of God in granting me ye opportunities and ability for it. I have abundantly experienced his rich goodness in ye year past, he hath sent me in seasonable supplies and mercifully spared me and mine, Blessed be his Name! O for a more humble and thankful heart, and O that I may live a more fruitful life.

Jan. 23rd. I visited William Ffoxlowe (at Tideswell) again and some others and returned to Fford at noon. Met my wife and other friends there, and dined with Mr. Bagshaw and returned. I have now advice that ye Prosecution begun against me by ye Churchwardens, and carried on in ye Spiritual Court, is dismissed ye Court. Blessed be God who hath not suffered my enemies to triumph.

Febry. 1st. I set out for Disley to endeavour to put an end to a Law-suit that had long been depending between Mary

(22). "In the Ecclesiastical Government of Villages there is the Parson or Vicar who hath Curam Animarum, the cure of souls (as the Lord of the Manour hath in some measure Curam Corporum), for which he hath the Tythes, Glebe and Church Offerings, hath under him the Church-wardens and Sidesmen to take care of the Church and Church Assemblies, the Overseers of the Poor, sick, aged and Orphane; and lastly the Clark to wait on him at Divine Service." In the Ecclesiastic Courts the process was by citation, then Bill and Answer.—The Present State of England, by Edw, Chamberlayne, LL.D., 1671.

Bradbury and Mary Kenion. Met Mr. Richardson at Disley, debated the matter til late. Came near an agreement but could not finish it. I returned with Mr Bardsley. Called awhile at Chappel. Got home safe.

Febry. 13th. At home before noon writing. In the afternoon Mr. Thos. Kyrke and J. Ashton called on me to accompany them to Fford. I spent some time with Mr. Bagshaw, and that night he set out for Derby to consult with other gentlemen about ye Election.

March 1st. Went up to Chappel to meet Mr. Bagshaw, Mr. Barker and others to consult about the ensuing Election, but stay'd not long.

March 6th. I had 5 teams from Chinley side to plow for us and we had a very favourable day. I rid over to see Katherine Brocklehurst at Overton, who is ill of an ague. Called on Francis Thomason and returned at even and went to bed much fatigued; but about midnight was called up by a messenger to my daughter (at Heafield) who was not expected to continue til I could come to her, and I set out and found her weak indeed, but some little recruited.

March 8th. I rid over to Heafield again on the same account, and had some little hope that Ann might recover. As I returned . I called at Chinley End, and met with Justice Bagshaw and Mr. Bagshaw of Fford who were treating ye ffreeholders there.

March 27th. I writ to Mr. Mills of Leek about ye abuses of ye Parish by ye Churchwardens, &c. (23.)

1734, April 2nd. I was called to Macclesfield to Mr. Eddowes, dangerously ill of Pthisis pulm: Dined at Mr. Acton's,

(23). The abuse of Church money by the wardens seems to have created quite a scandal in the parish. Certainly the accounts rendered by them disclose some curious items of expenditure which could not with reason be debited as Church expenditure. Their loyalty was superabundant to judge by the Royal birthdays it was thought necessary to celebrate. Look at the following items in the churchwardens' accounts for 1731:—

| | £ | s. | d. |
|---|---|---|---|
| June 11. Spent upon our Ringers and freeholders in our parish, being the King's Inaugurans | 0 | 5 | 0 |
| July 17. Spent at Rush-bearing | 0 | 4 | 4 |
| Oct. 23. Spent upon the King's Coronation Day | 0 | 5 | 0 |
| Oct. 30. Spent as usual being the King's Birthday | 0 | 5 | 0 |
| Oct. 28. Spent as usual being Princess Ann's Birthday | 0 | 5 | 0 |
| Dec. 7. Spent as usual being Princess Louisa's Birthday | 0 | 5 | 0 |
| Jan. 19th. Spent as usual being Prince Frederick's Birthday | 0 | 5 | 0 |
| March 1st. Spent as usual being Her Majesty's Birthday | 0 | 5 | 0 |
| May 29th. Spent as usual being the King's Restoration | 0 | 5 | 0 |
| May 30th. Spent as usual being Princess Chalolina's Birthday | 0 | 5 | 0 |
| N.D. Paid for a fox head | 0 | 1 | 0 |
| N.D. Paid for six badgers' heads | 0 | 6 | 0 |
| N.D. Paid for hedgehogs and Ravens | 1 | 4 | 3 |
| N.D. Paid for six Sacrament dinners as usual | 0 | 6 | 0 |
| Dec. 30th. Paid Geo. Bramwell tho Saxon one year's wages | 0 | 10 | 0 |

prescribed to Mr. Eddowes; sat awhile with Commissary Davenport and other friends. Lay at Mr. Acton's.

April 3rd. Visited Mr. Eddowes again and prescribed for him and Mrs. Acton. Dined at Mr. Acton's, and soon after set out for home. The weather has been favourable and this ride has done me good.

April 4th. Mr. Tricket is now prosecuting ye curate for immoralities. I could have wished he had not begun it; it creates much ill will, tho' no dissenter besides has any concern in ye prosecution. A Commission is now sitting at Buxton to examine Witnesses.

April 16th. At home til afternoon, then went up to be present at ye choice of Churchwardens; endeavoured to heal ye breach, but could not prevail; paid ye Church levies, but stayed too late in ye town.

May 15th. Set out for Derby in company with many neighbours. We entered Derby about 800 strong to vote for Lord Cavendish. The town was full of rioters, but I had no affront or disturbance.

May 16th. I visited the barrs where ye votes were taken, and visited several friends, and had advice on my vote but did not think fit to give it that day.

May 17th. I discoursed the matter more fully with Mr. Shaw, and was satisfied as to ye legality of my vote and gave it for Lord Charles, and afternoon set out for home, but my horse was hurt, and I left him at Duffield and lodged at Alport. (24.)

May 18th. Came to Tideswell and attended the funeral of my dear friend Mrs. Cresswell.

May 22nd. Dined at Fford. Heard from Derby the good news that Lord Charles Cavendish hath carried ye Election and that Sir Nath. Curzon is also come in, but it was an hard struggle.

---

(24). 1734. Election of Lord Charles Cavendish and Sir Nathaniel Curzon, Bart., as Knights of the Shire. The Candidates were Lord Chas. Cavendish, Sir Nath. Curzon, and Henry Harpur Esqre. There was a spirited contest; the object of the Tories was to turn out Lord Charles. The Election lasted from the 16th to the 23rd of May, and the numbers at the close were

| | |
|---|---|
| Lord Chas. Cavendish | 2081 |
| Sir Nath. Curzon | 2043 |
| Henry Harpur Esqre. | 1796 |

The mob became outrageous at the success of Cavendish; the people assembled before the County Hall and opposed his being chaired. A conflict occurred between his adherents and those of the other party. A great deal of mischief ensued, windows were broken and several persons were seriously injured and several wounded; a man had a sharp stick thrust into his eye as he endeavoured to prevent the crowd from entering the gate of the County Hall yard, and the injury caused his death.

May 27th.   A messenger came to call me to Derby to old Francis Thomason, seized with pleuritic fever there at the Election.   I set out with my wife for Tideswell, dined and left her there.   Set out for Derby about three in the afternoon, was at Derby about eight, and found my friend very weak.

May 28th.   Francis had got good rest and was better.   I visited Mr. Rogerson's family, consulted with Dr. Edwards about my friends case, and near noon set out.   Dined at Mrs. Hackers at Duffield and came to Tideswell about nine at night.   I called also at Wirksworth and Ashford.

May 29th.   I settled some affairs at Tideswell, boarded Alice Hill at Mr. Slaters, and after dinner set out with my wife for home, where we came safe in good time.   Blessed be God our Preserver!   We found Mrs. Sleigh of Chesterfield at our house, she came ye night before, to go through a course of Physick here for melancholic disorders.   May God grant us the desired success!

June 29th.   I find myself much indisposed and inclined to melancholy, occasioned by threats given out to prosecute me for voting at ye Election.   I did not vote rashly, I consulted several friends and in particular Mr. Shaw, who told me he had the opinion of Mr. Burrowes, a Councellor of their town.   I acquainted him with the whole of the case, and he told me I had a good right to vote, and I was persuaded I had so when I gave my vote.   I did not act against conscience in it, and this gives encouragement to hope that God will protect and deliver me.

June 30th.   I preached twice, as usual, from I. Peter 5, 8, and catechized twice.   Ye young men that learn to sing begun to perform yr parts.

July 8th.   I rid to Disley with widow Kenion to put an end to a lawsuit that had been carried on at times for 24 years.   The agreement was made, but I thought on hard terms for ye poor widow.

June 21st.   We had a very full congregation in the afternoon ; ye discourses were plain and practical and I hope of use. This night I received 9 pounds from Derby, part for myselfe and part for other Ministers, the gift of a person unknown at Edmonton.

July 29th.   Called at Slack Hall, met Joshua Wood there and had some discourse with him.   He owned some faults for which I had reproved him by a letter, but seemed stil' very highly displeased.   God teach him humility.

Aug. 4th.   Having this day been renewing my covenant with God, I have been thinking how I may do more for God and ye Salvation of ye souls Christ has purchased, than I have done. Alas! its but little very little that I have done.   I have lately been reading Dr. Calamy's account of the ejected Ministers, and there I see how far the Ministers of this age fall short of those in zeal, diligence and labour; when I read what pains they took in studying, in preaching in season and out, in visiting, catechizing, and teaching from house to house, in travelling day and night, in watching and fasting and fervent prayer; how purely how holily, how strictly they walked and lived; it fills me with shame and grief to think how little I have done and how loosely I have lived. My practice of Physick I find has taken up much of my time and costs me a good deal of pains, and I hope I do some service that way to God and my neighbour. But that is not the work I was chiefly devoted to, my Ordination vows are still upon me and I ought to take more pains for the salvation of souls, and to lay myself out more for promoting ye edification and salvation of those that are committed to my care, and of whom I must give an account; and this I purpose now thro Gods gracious assistance (which I humbly beg and hope for) to do. My purpose is

1st. To visit my people at their houses more frequently, and endeavour to make all my visits more useful to the souls there.

2nd. To encourage and frequent as often as I can meetings for prayer and conference at private houses, and to endeavour to bring in ye young persons of ye congregation to them.

3rd. To write more frequently serious letters at my hours of leisure to my children, my relations, and christian friends. Perhaps some good may be done that way, and I'm sensible its what I have hitherto too much neglected. O had I but a more fervent love to God and my Redeemer who loved and died for me!

Aug. 8th. At home till noon under some uneasiness to hear tidings from Derby, and I heard from Mr. Ash that Lord Charles and Sir Nath Curzon agreed well, and we hope that there will be no further strife or disturbance on account of ye Election.

Aug. 9th. I rid over to Heafield to see my daughter. I paid her husband 20 pounds, which, with what they had before, makes 50 pounds—the portion I promised her.

Sept. 29th. I preached twice (at Knutsford) from I. Tim. 1, 16. In the evening the congregation presented me by the hands of Sir Charles Duckinfield with a written call to be their pastor, signed by above an hundred; they told me it was an unanimous call, there not being one dissenting from it in the congregation. I desired a month's time to consider of it before I returned an answer, and it was agreed to. I lay that night at Sir Charles's at Tabley. (25.)

Sept. 30. I set out from Tabley with Mr. Holland and Mr. Potts, called at Knutsford, dined with Mr. Potts at Ollerton,

(25). Sir Charles Dukinfield, 2nd Bart., lived for many years at Macclesfield, from 1700 to 1720. Died 25th Febry., 1741-2, married the heiress of Sir Saml. Daniel, of Tabley.

and lay at Macclesfield at Mr. Culcheth's, after I had taken leave of Mr. Acton, who was to set out next morning for London.

Oct. 1st. I set out with Mr. Culcheth and Mr. Heald for Buxton, where ye Trustees met. I preached from Prov. 3, 6. We dined at The Hall, and agreed that Mr. Crowder should leave that place, the small congregation being lost and gone off. I returned home at night in a bitter tempest of rain and wind and was much fatigued.

Oct. 7th. At home reading Burnet de Statu Mortuorum et Resurgentium. Ye day exceeding stormy, wind and rain.

Oct. 10th. Many of the congregation met at my house, examined our title to ye place of worship and found it good, chose some new Trustees, and then debated the matter of my call to Knutsford. A promise was urged I made when called to Newcastle, but I made it appear ye conditions had never been performed. They promised they should be for the future, and some methods were proposed for that purpose. We dined together and parted in peace. Blessed be God.

Oct. 28th. I spent ye morning at home, and in the evening walked up to see Mrs. Clowes. I have for some days had a daughter of Mrs. Cresswell with me, and one of Mr. Crossland's. It grieves me to see how the poor creatures are neglected in yr education. What poor, foolish, ignorant, untaught creatures they are. If I must not do my duty to Mrs. Cresswell's children I will not act as executor.

Oct. 31st. Peter Wood came up to consult me what to do about his wife. Divine Providence hath at last discovered that she has for some years lived in adultery with a wicked wretch called Will. Fox who had before debauched Ellen Ward. This is likely to bring on us, and on the good ways of God, very great reproach. She formerly behaved well, was catechized and admitted to the Lord's Supper, and I had good hopes of her, but I fear the love of strong liquors hath ruined her.

Nov. 7th. My man sold a cow at the fair for 2£ 15s.

Nov. 11th. Walked up to Chappel, had some talk with ye curate about accommodating the controversies in the parish, to which he seems inclined at present if it hold.

Nov. 16th. Went to Peter Wood's, and according to my ability reproved and admonished his wife, laying open the heinousness of her crime. She expressed much sorrow and contrition. I sharply reproved the maid Priscilla for concealing the wickedness so long, and then returned to my work, and was obliged to sit up late.

Nov. 17th. I preached both parts of ye day from 2 Thes. 3, 1, and at night publickly expressed our detestation of the wickedness committed by W. Fox and Alice Wood, warning ye congregation to avoid him, and declaring her suspended from the Lords Table till we had grounds to hope that her repentance was sincere.

Dec. 5th. This night the neighbours were alarmed and called out to seek John Lingard, our neighbour, who had got too much drink and was missing, but found at last in a sorry condition.

Dec. 13th. I set out for Edale, dined at Carr, then visited my brother. A violent storm of wind and snow came on, which detained me all night. In my way back to Carr, I had a merciful deliverance from danger of being drowned. May I never forget Gods goodness in it. I lay this night at father Champions.

Dec. 14th. I visited brother Champion again, and then set out for home, but had a most stormy passage. The wind and snow beat in my face so furiously as brought me into danger.

1734-5. Jan. 6th. At night I had about 30 of our young people to supper. Many of them were young men learning Psalmody.

Jan. 25th. This day the Parish Officers sent me a Parish prentice, a poor child of Nicholas Longston's. This is a token of yr enmity, for, as far as I can hear, I ought not to have one. (26.)

Febry. 5th. I set out for Crich, dined at Baslow with brother and sister Thacker and brother Jephson. A kind Providence directed me safely over the East Moor, and I got in in good time.

Febry, 6th. I prescribed to ye young lady Mrs. Wilson, daughter to Mr. Wilson, Rector of St. Peter's in Nottingham, grand daughter of Dr. Wilson, Archdeacon of Coventry and Rector of Morley. She has been long ill and been under the care of many Physitians. May God prosper my endeavours! (27.)

Feb. 18th. I set out for Tideswell to ye auction of our

---

(26). The churchwardens and overseers of the poor with the consent of two Justices might bind any child whose parents they judged unable to maintain it, as an apprentice to any person who by his profession and manner of living had occasion to keep servants; and if such person was dissatisfied he might appeal to the sessions. Ministers of religion were not exempt from this imposition.

(27). In Morley Church, Derbyshire, there is a monument with the following inscription:—

"Here lie the bodies of the Revd. William Wilson M.A., late Archdeacon of Coventry and Rector of this Church, who died May ye 11th 1741, aged 95. And Elionora his wife who died Oct. 24th 1707, Also William, George and Ann their Grand children."

Society books, and lay at Mr. Kelsal's. I bought a considerable parcel of them.

1735, March 27th. Went on to Manchester and lay at my son's. Had some serious talk with John about his affair, and found him too much set upon it.

March 28th. I visited and prayed with my sister, and then went to Mr. Evans's, and sent him for Mr. Parks the young womans father, but he refused to come, and sufficiently expressed his aversion to ye match. I returned to my son's, and gave John a solemn charge not to marry without my consent and the consent of her father. He promised to delay it awhile, and that was all I could bring him to.

April 3rd. Hired Ffrancis Dean, am to give him five pounds per annum and his vails and cloath for a shirt. He comes at May Day.

April 10th. I set out early for Ashford (from Crich). Had a guide but we lost our way in a close mist, but a kind Providence directed me safe off the High Moor.

April 12th. Something interrupted by persons who came for advice. This day I hear Mr. Eyre of Stockport is dead. I had a familiar acquaintance with him. He had left the Dissenters, made push in trade to get an estate, but lived too fast and broke a good constitution, and died of universal decay; in what condition I dont hear.

May 29th (Manchester). We had some talk with Mrs. Bent, with whom we agreed for teaching ye girls. Bought some books and dined, and intended to set out for home, but were over-persuaded by friends to stay another night, and spent most of ye afternoon at ye bowling green.

June 5th. This night I had a letter from Dr. Saml. Wright of London, granting me a considerable share in a charitable bequest. Blessed be God for this unexpected favour!

June 12th. I set out for Derby; Mr. Kelsal and Mr. Fletcher accompanied me. We dined at Mr. Roberts's at Alport, baited again at Kirk Ireton, came to Derby in good time. Mr. Rogerson supped with us and we despatched what business we had and went to bed.

June 13th. Early in the morning I was seized with a painful fitt of ye strangury. I thought it owing to our late supper and some hard beer, but it went off before noon. We visited Mr. Shaw and Mr. Crompton and I called on Mr. Bateman. We then set out for Morley. I visited Mrs. Wilson and dined with her and her grandfather the Archdeacon of Coventry. Viewed ye monuments in ye Church, and went on by Belper to Matlock Bath, bathed there and lay there all night.

June 16th. I walked over to Fford to visit the family there and see Mr. Ash. I supped with the family and returned in good time. I called to see Mrs. Smith; found Madam Bagshaw there, who told me that that morning their gardener lay longer than usual in bed, on account of a bad wound in his leg. That about six in ye morning ye gardener saw Mr. Ash come into ye room he lay in, he came to ye bed and asked him many questions, then walked to ye window, took up a book that lay there, and looked in it awhile, having nothing on but his shirt and his night cap, then walked off. A little boy that lay in ye room, nephew to Mr. Bagshaw, affirms that he also saw and heard all this; Mr. Ash affirms that he was never out of his room that morning til eight o'clock, that he slept well all night, found the door made, when he dressed and came down, as he made it ye night before, and that he never walked in his sleep in all his life. What shall we say to this but wait for the event.

June 21st. Mr. Holland and Mr. Hardman were with me this morning and sat about an hour. My man came back at night, brought me no bad tidings from my children, but ye sad news that my friend and bookseller Robt. Whitworth of Manchester is apprehended and sent to Lancaster for vending false stamps and his life is in danger. (28.)

July 2nd. Rid over to Tideswell and was terribly beaten by wind and rain; dined with Mr. Kelsal, there appealed to ye Justices about my apprentice, and they gave it on my side, I returned safe in the evening. Blessed be God!

July 15th. I set out for the Sessions at Bakewell with Jos. Wood, called at Tideswell but did not alight. Was very much wet before I got to Bakewell. Retained Mr. Cook for my counsel. Dined in ye room with ye Justices and went up to ye Court, and after a brisk trial I carried my cause and got quit of ye burden of an apprentice.

July 17th. (Tideswell). Set out with Mr. Kelsal for the visitation. Got our business despatched forthwith. Went up to ye Church, Mr. Groves preached a good sermon. Our parish had a long trial about Churchwardens and our friends lost it. The antient custom was broke through by ye Dean against all right and law.

Aug. 7th. I had an unhappy difference with my wife and uttered some harsh and hasty expressions yt cost me trouble after, God grant me meekness and humility, may I learn of Jesus!

(28). Robert Whitworth, of Cockpit Hill, Manchester, was one of the principal publishers and stationers in the North of England.

Sept. 29th. Set out for Chesterfield with dear John Cross-well, called at Tideswell, and dined at Stoney Middleton, and lodged at Mr. Slater's in Chesterfield. Found my son John in pretty good health.

Sept. 30th. Set out for Gainsborough. Dined at Worksop and came to Gainsborough in good time, and found my good friend Mrs. Jackson in health, and lodged there.

Oct. 1st. Visited Mrs. Rudsdale, and Mrs. Robinson and Mr. Flower in ye morning. Dined with a good deal of company at Mr. Coles, and then went to see Dr. Huntington.

Oct. 2nd. It was heavy rain, which obliged us to stay another day. Mr. Rudsdale returned from Lincoln and was with us most of ye day. We dined at Madam Jacksons and supped there too, and were too magnificently treated. I went with Mr. Rudsdale to sit with Mr. Flower and Madam Hopkinson, prayed with them and took leave near bedtime.

Oct. 3rd. Came safe to Chesterfield, where we hear the afflicting tidings of ye sudden death of my dearest friend and brother Mr. Ashe.

Oct. 20th. This day I set out for Leek, ye road was in many places exceeding bad, but I came thither in safety about 2 hours past noon. Visited Mr. Daybanks sons, found one in an hopeful way, ye other past recovery. Spent some time with Mr. Charles Potts and lodged at Mr. Worthington's house.

Oct. 21st. Visited and prescribed for ye boy but with little hopes of success. Visited Mrs. Mills. Called to Mrs. Davison ill of cancer in ye breast, recommended her to Dr. White. Spent part of ye day at Mr. Robinson's, and ye evening with Mr. Worthington and Mr. Wheelwright from Stone in Staffordshire.

Oct. 22nd. Visited Mrs. Robinson and Mrs. Davison ; the older of Mr. Daybanks sons died this morning, the other continues hopeful. I set out for Ashford, lost my way, but came safe thither about 2 afternoon. Fell to ye prizing of Mr. Ashe's books, and continued at work til' ten, then spent some time with Mr. Harris and Mr. Bennett about fixing a minister in that place.

Oct. 23rd. I went to work again prizing books till after ten o'clock. Then set out for Tideswell and dined there. A messenger came to call me to Constance ye daughter of John Wright, dangerously ill of ye small-pox.

Oct. 25th. Last night a letter came from Mr. Wildman with advice that by his interest he had procured me a share in the legacy of Mrs. Read of Hackney. 10 pounds.

Dec. 8th. Rid over to Buxton to see John Wainwright's wife, deeply melancholy. Returned at night with Mr. Arnold Kyrke ; I never travelled on a worse road.

Dec. 9th. My good old mare was found dead this morning.

1735-6. February 1st. Preached only once from Gen. 3, 12, 13. Continued in ye pulpit about three hours.

Feb. 10th. I was called out to Bowden Head and to Slack Hall. Dined at Fford, walked after to ye Overfold and Gorsty Low. Then home and after that to Blackbrook. The snow was deep and I was much fatigued, and when I came last home got a fall in ye house by a slip, that over-stretched ye tendons in my leg and thigh and gave me much pain, and I fear will for some time disable me from walking so well as I could before.

February 14th. At home all day preparing sermons. My wife called out to a sinful creature in travail. God give her repentance !

Febry. 15th. Preached twice as usual, the way was very bad and few at a distance could attend. Some agents from the Grecian Churches were this day at Chappel-le-Frith. They are going about for reliefe for those distressed Christians.

March 1st. I sett out with Mr. Bagshaw for Macclesfield, to prevail with Commisary Davenport to undertake ye discharge of Saml Bagshaw now at Gibraltar. There were great rejoicings, it was ye Queens birthday. (29.)

March 10th. An antient man came for advice and brought a water from beyond Southwel in Nottinghamshire, on foot, about 36 miles.

1736, March 26th. Walked to Town End to meet ye London carrier, who brought down Mr. Ashe's funeral sermon and ye account of his life printed, and some other books which I had sent for. (30.)

---

(29). Commissary Davenport was Peter Davenport, Esq., created about 1740 Sir Peter Davenport ; married 1st Mary d. of Edw. Thornicroft, Esq., of Macclesfield, ob. 18th, 1718.
2nd, Miss Lucy Frances Legh, d. of Colonel Legh, of Adlington, Nov., 1723.
3rdly, Mary, widow of Wm. Dukinfield, Esq., of Castle Hill, Dukinfield.
Sir Peter Davenport died intestate, and was buried at Prestbury, 27th Jan., 1746-7, leaving an only daughter, Elizabeth. He lived in Macclesfield in a large house in King Edward Street. The young Pretender stayed there in '45, and it was afterwards purchased for the Grammar School as a residence for the headmaster.

(30.) Dr. Clegg edited several books which were published in London, viz :—
A rather thin small 8vo. volume entitled "Essays on Union to Christ," by the Apostle of the Peak, which was published after his decease by the

April 2nd. I baptized a young man at Ashford yesterday. His father was an Anabaptist, but willing he should be baptized by me, and his mother much desired it. He seemed a modest young man, and to be serious and well disposed.

May 10th. I set out for home (from Manchester), was by the way called to see a child of Francis Thomason. When I was got on horseback to return, in passing through a yate, an iron hook it was hasped with catched hold on my great coat and stuck through ye top of my strong boot, and ye mare rushing forward from under mee, I fell on my head and shoulder to the ground with great violence, the rest of my Body hung by my Boot on ye Hook. I was stunned with ye fall. Francis Thomason with difficulty disengaged me, and I mounted again and came home, much pained in my head and shoulder. This was a great and remarkable deliverance; I desire I may never forget it. Blessed be God for this merciful and seasonable appearance for me.

May 11th. Visited Mrs. Wingfield at Fford. She gave me four guineas and sent two to my wife.

May 12th. I set out for Macclesfield, came there about 10. Prescribed to Mrs. Heald and then set out for Leek, dined there and went on to Ashbourne and lay there all night, much fatigued.

May 13th. Set out for Derby, got there about nine. Preached there from Eccles vi., 12. A great number of Ministers were there. We settled ye matters relating to ye intended Ordination, and adjusted ye distribution of ye fund moneys, and I returned with Mr. Kelsal and Mr. Fletcher to Matlock Bath, and there we lodged.

May 14th. I set out for home. Dined at Alport. Visited Mr. Mather called at Tideswell and came safe home thro ye favour of a kind Providence.

Rev. John Ashe and Dr. Clegg, who jointly wrote the Epistle Dedicatory. "Printed in London for Nevil Simmons, bookseller at Sheffield, 1705." Dr. Clegg wrote also "The Scripture Account of the Covenants and the interest of Faith in Justification briefly explained and vindicated in some Remarks on Mr. Saml. de la Rose's Brief Account of the Two Covenants in a letter to a friend in Stockport. London, Printed by J. Noon in Cheapside near Mercers Chappel, 1722, 8vo." Also "Sermon preached by the Revd. Dr. Clegg at the Ordination of Mr. John Holland, jr., at Chesterfield, Aug. 11th, 1731, with an exhortation delivered by the Revd. John Ashe." Probably printed for J. Noon aforesaid, 1731, 8vo. Also "A discourse occasioned by the sudden death of the Revd. Mr. John Ashe of Ashford in the Peak. To which is added a short account of his life and character, and of some others in or near the High Peak in Derbyshire. As an appendix to the Revd. Wm. Bagshaw's Book de Spiritualibus Pecci, London. Printed for J. Noon at the White Hart in Cheapside near Mercers Chappel, 1736. Small 8vo." Also "Seventeen Sermons by the late Revd. Mr. John Ashe of Ashford in the High Peak, with a preface by the Revd. J Clegg. London, sold by J. Noon at the White Hart near Mercers Chappel in Cheapside, Mr. Jonathan Slater in Chesterfield, Mr. Jer. Roe in Derby, and Mr. John Simmons in Sheffield, 1741. 8vo."

May 19th. Called at John Fieldings to see ye afflicted family; had some discourse with the son and daughter that are disordered by melancholy.

May 29th. I hear that Mr. Tricket is cast in ye suit which he commenced against our Curate, contrary to ye advice of all his friends. This I fear may be of bad consequence to ye dissenting interest in these parts.

June 9th. I went to Malcoffe to visit Grace Young, who was under great concern about her nephew Mr. Tricket, who, thro' the perjury of ye witness who swore against him, has been cast in ye suit he commenced against ye Curate, on which account there has been wild and wicked rioting and revelling at Chappel-en-le-Frith.

June 28th. Set out for Tideswell. Mr. Ashe's books were sold by auction. Ye auction continued til' midnight and we sat up late.

June 29th. At the Auction again, which continued til' after midnight, and we did not part til' 2 hours after that.

July 26th. Several Ministers came and supped with me.

July 27th. Many more Ministers came, and about 10 we went to ye Chappel. Mr. Worthington of Dean Row began with prayer and reading ye Scriptures. A Psalm was sung. Mr. Turner of Knutsford prayed, Mr. Eaton of Allostock preached from Prov. II., 30, an excellent serious sermon. Mr. Culch.th received ye confessions and proposed the questions and prayed over Mr. Kelsal, Mr. Whittaker prayed over Mr. Fletcher, and I gave ye exhortation and concluded with prayer. Vast numbers attended, and blessed be God that no disaster befell any. Ye Ministers dined with me, 17 in number, and several other friends.

Sept. 6th. Afternoon I went out to Malcoffe and Fford, laboured in vain to heal a breach between Mr. Bagshaw and Mr. Tricket. Was applied to for medicines by a young woman, servant to Mrs. Young. I suspect she is with child and yt she wants it to be destroyed.

Sept. 10th. I set out for Gainsborough; called and dined at Tideswell, and came to Chesterfield in good time. Lodgd at Mr. R. Slaters. Hear that Mr. Whites young child is seized with the small-pox.

Sept. 11th. Visited some friends. Rid over to Calow and found ye child exceeding full of small-pox of a bad kind and in danger. I prescribed for it and lodged there all night.

Sept. 16th. The night past very rainy and the wind high. When it began to clear up I set out for Gainsborough, dined at

Retford, and came safe through ye mercy of God to Madam Jacksons house in very good time and lodged there.

Sept. 17th. Rid out with the company to Paddocks, where we spent the day in reading and diversions and returned without misfortune.

Oct. 5th. Thomas Cresswells wife came with a bill from her husband for 3 guineas which I paid her. Soon after came Mr. Kelsal's brother and told me Thomas Cresswell had deserted ye Army and was at his house in Cheshire in a poor condition.

Oct. 12th. (In Manchester.) Thomas Cresswell came to us. I proposed to him to return to the Regiment, and undertook to procure his pardon, Commissary Davenport having promised it; but he absolutely refused, and resolved to go to sea, and Mr. Kelsall has gone along with him to Leverpool.

Oct. 21st. Went up to town on business about my cattle, which I was told had been arrested on account of rent due from the person I had laid them to, but a merciful Providence prevented disturbance.

Dec. 11th. I settled accounts with ye dancing master, and paid that moneys with a grumbling conscience, and am resolved never to pay more on that account.

Dec. 12th. I preached only once, but was in the pulpit about 3 hours, and was mercifully assisted and strengthened and was not much fatigued.

Dec. 20th. At home all day. Reading Oldmixon's Hist: of K. William and Q. Anne til' late.

1736-7, Jan. 17th. Walked over to Fford to see Mrs. Bagshaw, who was ill of the common disorder, returned by Malcoffe. We have heard of many sad disasters that have befallen several persons about us; one in Edale was shot accidentally thro' the leg, and ye part so shattered that it is taken off. Another in ye Peak Forest was going about to collect ye Land Tax on the Lords Day, fell from a wall yt he was climbing over, and was so bruised that he shortly died of it. Ellis Needham of Castleton thrown off his horse and dangerously hurt, and his man about the same time broke his thigh. A Clergyman of Motterham, disordered as we hear by drink, fell from his horse and has not been able to speak since. These are warnings against sinful practices, and to all to be ready.

Jan. 20th. Heard ye news of ye Kings safe arrival.

Jan. 27th. I was at a fair at Chappel and sold two young bullocks.

Febry. 18th. About three o'clock the sun was eclipsed, very visible.

March 2nd. We had 6 teams came to plow for us. They did a great deal of work and did it well, and blessed be God no disaster befell any of them.

1737, May 3rd. Set out with Mr. Culcheth and Mr. Heald for Knutsford, to the meeting of the Cheshire Ministers. Mr. Turner prayed. I preached from I Cor. 9, 27. Several gross immoralities committed by Mr. David Herbert were complained of to the Ministers, and clear and full proof of ye facts appearing, he was by them disowned and rejected, and a letter ordered to be written to his hearers to withdraw from him as one yt walked very disorderly.

Augst. 17th. Our honoured father was interred in the Churchyard at Roachdale. I preached after at ye Meeting place.

Augst. 24th. I designed this day to have set out for Gainsborough, but some indisposition and ye uncertainty of ye weather discouraged me, and I was not willing to leave so much of our corn standing. I was at home with ye reapers.

Augst. 29th. I set out for Knutsford, being called to see Mr. Turner the Minister there, dangerously ill of a complicated disorder. I called at Macclesfield, dined with Dr. Colthurst at Sandlebridge, and went on with ye Doctor to Knutsford. We prescribed to Mr. Turner, sat awhile with Mr. Sidebottom, and returned to Sandlebridge.

Sept. 1st. I set out with my friends (Mr. Hamilton and Mrs. Berry) for Buxton, dined there, and spent ye afternoon there in cheerfulness, and returned.

Sept. 2nd. I set out with Mr. Hamilton, and Mrs. Berry for Castleton to see yt wonder. We dined there and returned in good time. (30A.)

Sept. 13th. Called to William Heward of Charlsworth, dangerously ill of ye Cholera Morbus. Dined at Park Hall, and called at Jos. Hadfields in my return, where I found my wife visiting.

Sept. 19th. (At Gainsborough.) I had a letter from Mr. Eaton inviting me to take Nottingham on my way, but my companion (Mr. Tricket) was so unhappily mounted that he could not go with me, nor could I leave him.

Oct. 6th. We had a fair at Chappel. I sold an old mare

(30A). "Yt Wonder" at Castleton was the Peak Cavern, which was one of the Seven Wonders of the Peak.

for 2 guineas and a young one for 3£ 10s., and returned in good time.

Oct. 10th.  Called to ye funeral of George Low of Oldenshaw, who went out well on ye Fryday morning before, and was found dead in ye field soon after.  Some suppose him to have been killed by his horse.

Nov. 25th.  I heard of the death of our most excellent Queen. Its a great and sad breach in ye nation.  May we all lay it to heart and duly lament the sins that provoked God to make it. (31.)

Dec. 5th.  Set out to see Sam. Needham's wife at Hucklow, afflicted with the Hysterick Colick.

Dec. 17th.  I prepared a sermon from Rev. 3, 3, and gave a briefe Repetition of the substance of many of ye discourses that had been delivered this year.

Dec. 18th.  I delivered the Repetition Sermon to a pretty full congregation.

Dec. 22nd.  Went up to Chappel to settle matters with him about ye Lawsuits, had same hott words with him about his bill, which cost me much concern after.  I have not that rule over my own spirit that I recommend to others.  May God teach me more meekness and humility and watchfulness.

1737-8.  Jan. 2nd.  I was called to a woman that was housekeeper for Wm. Carrington at Ashton Clough.  They told me she was ill of ye colick, but I found her in labour.

Jan. 10th.  I was at home all day, a great deal of snow fell. I spent most of it in reading ye Martyrology.

Jan. 18th.  Continued diverting ourselves (at Tideswell). Dined at Mr. Kelsals, supped at Mr. Hadfields, where we stayed up too late and spent not ye time so well as the night before. Good Lord pardon our vanity.

Jan. 27th.  Rid over to Chelmorton to baptize a child for Jos. Bott there, and purchased ye meeting place, of J. Buxton, for ye use of ye congregation there, ye price 8 pounds.

(31). Queen Caroline died on Sunday evening, Dec. 1st, 1737 (Nov. 20th O.S.).  Dr. Clegg's lamentations are a contrast to the well-known description of the Queen's deathbed by Carlyle.
"Little George blubbered a good deal, fidgeted and flustered a good deal, much put out, poor foolish little man.  The dying Caroline recommended HIM to Walpole, advised His Majesty to marry again.  ' Non, jaurai des Maitresses,' sobbed H.M. passionately.  ' Ah Mon Dieu cela n'empeche pas ' answered she from long experience of the case."

Jan. 31st. At home all day. Mrs. Young came to visit us and too much time was spent unprofitably with her.

Febry. 3rd. Rid over to Henry Marchingtons, baptized his child named James. Dined there, and in crossing over the pastures towards Ford lost my way and was in danger of being laid fast in ye bogs. It was a thick mist, but I came at last into the high road, and to Ford and safe home, D.G.

Feb. 18th. At home all day reading and writing. Called out of bed in ye night past to make up a medicine for Will. Bagshaw, Mr. Bagshaw's nephew, much bruized by the fall of an Ark lid upon him.

Febry. 22nd. After dinner I baptized the child of Ann Bradbury, after she had made an humble and penitent confession of her sin before several communicants and others of the Congregation. Called it Betty.

March 7th. Carried my wife to Ford; some friends met there to consult about the Parish Suit. We have notice given that the cause must be tried. I think our cause just. May God appear for us and give us success.

March 9th. Ye swine was killed. Lent Mr. Tricket 10 pounds.

March 13th. Mr. Tricket dined with me, he is very busy preparing for ye trial at Derby. Our adversaries seem confident, and some of our friends dejected, but God can turn the scales as he pleases; trust him.

March 17th. At night news came that ye Parish Cause was not tried, ye Judge could not stay, but our friends have a better heart of it.

1738, April 28th. I was called to baptize a child of John and Martha Marchington. They called it Samuel, for it had been asked of the Lord, they having been married fourteen years and not had any child before.

May 14th. In the forenoon whilst we were in the Chappel there was the heaviest shower of rain that I ever saw. The waters were raised in less than two hours to a prodigious height, and it was with difficulty that we got home at noon and returned after dinner.

June 2nd. I had a very merciful deliverance when mounting my mare.

June 4th. One of our Communicants, Jos. Hadfield, now absconds for debts which he has contracted, by which many are

I

sufferers, to the great scandal of our Society and Profession. . . . He has acted a most base and scandalous part.

June 16th. After dinner brother John and sister came to us, and many matters relating to my father and his will were debated with more passion than was becoming us. They are uneasy that I come in for an equal share of his estate. This reward I have for all that I have done for them.

June 26th. Set out for Goit Head; rid from thence to Buxton, met Mr. Culcheth and set out with him and Mr. Harrison. Called at Chelmorton to settle some matters about ye Meeting Place. Dined at Baslow and came to Chesterfield, where we saw many friends and took up our lodgings.

June 27th. Set out again, and dined at Mansfield, where we met some others of our Brethren and went on to Nottingham, and came in good time. Mr. Culcheth and I lodged at Dr. Eatons.

June 28th. Many Ministers assembled at ye High Pavement Meeting Place and a great Congregation. Mr. Rogerson began ye service. Mr. Culcheth prayed, and I preached from Rom. 14, 19. We dined together and were nobly treated. The Ministers, ye Mayor and many others unanimously requested that the sermon might be published, and I at last agreed to it, and delivered ye M.S. to Dr. Eaton.

June 29th. Dined with several other Brethren at Dr. Eatons; about four set out again, passed thro' Newark and lodged at Long Collingham.

June 30th. Set out early and came to Gainsborough about halfe an hour past nine in the morning; found our friends there most of them pretty well.

July 1st. We visited several friends, and in the afternoon went awhile a fishing in ye river Trent.

July 20th. Still busy in our hay. Several friends hereabouts called to the Assizes as Jurymen. The Parish trial is likely to come on.

July 25th. This night we hear we have lost ye cause at Derby.

July 26th. All the town at Chappel full of rioting and drunkeness on account of their victory at Derby.

Aug. 3rd. A messenger came to call me to Leek to Mrs. Wardle Boosely. I set out and got there about noon, but she was dead about a quarter of an hour before.

Augst. 15th. We began to cut our wheat.

Dec. 18th. Set some young elms in ye Chappel yard.

1738-9. January 4th. The day was very stormy and tempestuous, and in some parts there was very terrible thunder and lightning.

Jan. 22nd. The Trustees for Priestcliffe and Wormhill Schools came over, and I was with them at the Royal Oak til' far in ye afternoon. We settled that matter as well as we then could, and parted in peace.

Jan. 31st. A stormy day, with excessive rain that raised the waters to a prodigious height in the night.

Febry. 1st. There was a fair at Chappel, but few cattle could be brought to it, ye waters were so high.

March 13th. A barrel of oysters was sent to me from London by Mr. Peters.

1739. April 3rd. Ye wind in ye North and ye weather exceeding cold with snow and sleet. This permits us not to carry daughter Sally out into the air, which I think would conduce above all things to her recovery.

April 4th. Sent away some of Mr. Doddridges Family Expositor just published.

April 5th. Went up to meet some friends at Chappel in ye afternoon about our parish suits, and paid towards my share of the cost 14 pounds, which lies heavy on me.

April 22nd. This day brother Clegg acquaints me by ye Post with the death of my good old friend and brother Mr. Dawson, Minister at Roachdale. He had been Minister there 43 or 44 years, and after a holy and useful life died in great peace.

May 14th. Mr. Kelsal came over to consult what to do to vindicate his reputation from imputations cast upon him by a bad woman, and stayed most of ye day.

June 21st. Heard from my son Joseph at Portsmouth, and soon received the watch with which he has presented me, and which we feared had been lost.

July 11th. Rid over to Buxton with daughter Sally, lodged at Mr. Harrisons.

July 12th. Dined at Martinside, and came safe home, blessed be God, as we were in danger through the mare's boggling at ye carcass of a dead horse.

Augst. 12th. After Sermons read Mr. Whitfields Journal and was amazed to consider the work that man got through. He seems to me to have the true spirit of the Evangelist, only too full of himselfe and too enthusiastic.

Augst. 21st. We are taking ye roof off ye house. This day the Races begin and will take all off their work.

Sept. 4th. At home all day, writing a long letter to Dr. Eaton about some Doctrinal points we have different apprehensions of ; and sometimes with the workfolks.

Sept. 13th. Paid Mr. Bagshaw seven guineas towards Mr. Wildman's bill.

Sept. 8th. At home all the day, and spent it in fasting and prayer, and in the conclusion had great satisfaction in what I had done. May ye benefit be lasting.

Oct. 30th. I set out with Mr. Saml. Bagshaw for Tideswell, to receive rents and settle accounts relating to Thos. Cresswell and ye rest of ye children, and to end a controversie between Mrs. Hall and a man of Castleton, relating to some part of her Estate. It was referred to Mr. Markland, Vicar of Tideswell, and myselfe. We met and had long debates but could not come to any agreement.

Oct. 31st. Met again about ye Arbitration twice, but could not come to a conclusion of that, nor of ye accounts, so we were constrained to lodge at Tideswell again.

Nov. 1st. Began early to go on with ye accounts and ended about ten. Breakfasted at Mr. Hadfield's and then set out for home. This day Mrs. Elizabeth Touchet came to board with us. May it please God to make her stay with us agreeable and every way beneficial to her.

Nov. 2nd. About three I walked up to Chappel to meet ye persons concerned in ye Parish suits. I paid to the full this night all my share of the costs and charges of those suits, being in all above 27 pounds, and am fully determined never more to engage in any suits.

Nov. 5th. Set out for Tideswell. Met Mr. Markland there ; finished our Arbitration, but it was too late to return, so I lodged at Mr. Kelsals.

Nov. 9th. Mrs. Touchet got no sleep. Soon after midnight my daughter wakened me in a terrible fright, durst not stay in bed with her. In the morning she was very wild and frantick and so continued all the day.

Nov. 10th. Mrs. Touchet had a restless raving night, got no sleep at all, nor suffered any to sleep in the family, was quite frantick all ye day. I writ to her friends by ye post to fetch her away, my wife and daughters not being able to bear the disturbance by her cursing and swearing and frantick actions and expressions.

Nov. 14th. Mrs. T. rested some part of the night and we thought got some sleep, but in the morning was as wild and frantick as ever. This night a chaise came to take her home.

Nov. 15th. Mrs. T. had a raving night till almost morning, then lay still but we could not tell that she had any sleep.

Nov. 16th. Mrs. T. had a raving fitt that lasted from nine at night till one in the morning. I got up and called ye servants to bind her faster, she being set up in bed. This morning about ten ye chaise set out with her, and she behaved better than was expected at her going off; it was unhappy for us and much more for her to be seized with this disorder in my house, but Divine wisdom orders all well, and can bring good out of this evil both to her and to us.

Nov. 22nd. Much disturbed about an affair that Mr. Clegg, of Leverpool has engaged me in. I believe his intention in it is just and good, but I was afraid this might bring me into trouble and make some desperate persons my enemies. As Mr. Clegg is my friend, I desire to serve him as far as I can with a good conscience, and to commit myself to ye protection of God.

Dec. 3rd. Set out for Castleton, to put an end to ye controversy between Mrs. Hall and Staveley and did finish it, blessed be God! but not without difficulty.

Dec. 14th. At night my brother John Clegg called on us on his return from London and lodged with us. Blessed be God, my brother had been carried in safety up and down, and brings me very comfortable tidings from my son Joseph, for which I desire to be truly thankful. I once was afraid of great griefe and trouble in that child, but am now encouraged to hope for matter of rejoycing.

Dec. 17th. I had last night a very bad night; an ague fitt seized me, and then an high ffever; got little sleep and it did not refresh me. In ye morning I found myselfe almost disabled from walking and was full of pain. I took some powdered sulphur, and Balsam of sulphur mixed with conserve of roses, drinking after it whey and small liquors, but had a very bad day.

Dec. 18th. Had a very bad night, short sleeps and sadly perplexed and lost; my ffever was very high, great and continual thirst, but when I was up found my pain abated and was more able to walk, but had no appetite but to drink. I drank apple tea and small table beer, and a glass or two of birch wine, with a little claret, and before night found my ffever and thirst abating. My daughter read me Mr. Corbets Selfe Employment in Secret. I was pleased and I hope profited by it, tho' I found my heart too little answered ye account that good man gave of his. I found myselfe most defective in love to God and resignation to his will. O for a more humble and meek and heavenly heart.

Dec. 20th. Many poor came for relief. I love not to send any away empty. Blessed be God who has enabled me to give anything.

Dec. 30th. The wind was so high and ye cold so severe that in the forenoon I preached in my house. In the afternoon I preached at our Chappel but the wind had broke the windows very much, and blown down one of ye firr trees, and it was with great difficulty that we went out and returned.

Dec. 31st. The wind still very high with snow, and the frost ye keenest that ever was known in these parts in this age.

1739-40. Jan. 2nd. Spent ye evening with some young people at my house. Ye moon totally eclipsed this night.

Jan. 9th. Was the fast day. I was in the pulpit about 3 hours and tho' I had not tasted any food or liquor till 3 in ye afternoon, I found myselfe very fresh and strong.

Jan. 21st. The frost continues very sharp and severe. I am glad to hear of ye Charitable Collections in London and other parts for ye poor, and think myselfe now obliged to give something extraordinary for their reliefe. (32.)

1739-40, Jan. 22nd. I intended to visit Henry Mellor but could not pass thro' the drifts of snow.

March 7th. Finished the reading of Mr. Taylor's piece of Original Sin, and was well pleased with ye clearness of his reasoning, his candor and ye strain of piety and seriousness that runs through it, but am not thoroughly satisfied in all he advances.

March 16th. We hear that Admiral Vernon has taken Puerto Bello from ye Spaniards. Blessed be God for this success! (33.)

(32). This was the time when there was a great frost in London. It lasted nine weeks, and coaches plied upon the Thames and festivities and diversions of all kinds were enjoyed on the ice. The season was called "Ye hard Winter."

(33). Porto Bello captured by Admiral Vernon on the 21st November, 1739, with six men of war. An absurd fuss was made over this exploit, which was attended with little loss to our fleet, owing to political feeling, Vernon being opposed to Walpole.

1740, May 23rd. Called to a son of Wm. Shirt, an apprentice, who has lost the use of his lower parts by being rubbed with a mercurial ointment, and being starved after in ye cold season.

May 26. The wind very high in ye East and very cold. Ye drought stil' continues and threatens a scarcity. Mobbing and disturbances in several parts about us, to prevent ye carrying of meat out of ye Country. Lord pity ye poor and needy!

June 13th. (Nottingham.) Set out for Lincoln. Dined at Newark and came to Lincoln in good time and lay there.

June 14th. Spent about two hours in viewing ye Minster, that noble pile of building and its monuments; and then set out for Gainsborough and came safe thither about noon, and dined with Mr. Woodhouse.

June 17th. Set out for Hull, but lay that night at Brig.

June 18th. Came in good time to Barton and went off in a hoy for Hull. The wind was against us but by the mercy of God we got safe to shore. After we had seen ye Dock, ye Garrison, and the Man of War building there, &c., we left Hull and set out for Beverley, and came thither betwixt nine and ten at night.

June 19th. We got up pretty soon and took a view of the Minster. Its not near so large as that of Lincoln, but the building more neat and compact and uniform and much better kept. After breakfast we set out through Walkington, and thro' Hunsley, over Walling Ffen to Howden, and thence to Booth Ferry, to Airmin, and to Rawcliffe, where we dined and viewed the shipping there; and set out by Thorne, and over Hatfield Chase, to Hatfield, and to Doncaster and lodged at ye sign of ye Woolpack.

June 20th. We set out and travelled thro' Warmsworth and Conisborrough and Thribergh and Rotherham to Sheffield. Dined there and came safe home in good time and good health, and found my family in as comfortable circumstances as I left it. We met with kind reception among our friends and generous entertainment. Had fine roads and fine weather and met with no disaster by the way. God's name be ever praised.

June 21st. Mr. Goddard, Vicar of Glossop, called me up to Chappel to give an account of what I knew as to Mr. Froggat's last will and testament.

June 30th. Mr. Kelsal and Tom Cresswell came from Tideswell, and Mr. Charnel and Mr. Harrison from Buxton, and ye rest of the afternoon was spent in catching fish.

July 31st. I found myself better in the morning. I am intending by degrees to fall into a vegetable diet and to leave off all strong liquors, hoping it may be beneficial both to ye body and mind.

Oct. 7th. Walked over to Fford and dined with Mrs. Bagshaw. Stepd thence to John Ffielding's, his son Jeremy was very suddenly seized a little time before and found dead or dying in a field by the house. Ye young man had long been under sad disorder of mind and in danger of destroying himself or some others of ye family ; its a mercy yt both these evils were prevented.

Nov. 18th. This day ye Parliament meets, may the Divine blessing be upon all their Consultations. The Emperor of Germany and the Empress of Russia are dead. Blessed be God that our King is alive and in health. May he still be continued a blessing to us, and may all his endeavours for the Publick good be crowned with success. (34.)

Dec. 10th. At home til' afternoon, reading " Principles of Moral Philosophy."

Dec. 17th. At home all day reading. My man carrying coals to be given to our poor neighbours, this cold and uncomfortable season.

Dec. 31st. We had our neighbours to supper with us and spent some time, I hope, in innocent cheerfulness.

1740-1. Jan. 9th. Close at work all day and til' late at night in hard study, but I find this sinks my spirits.

Jan. 16th. At home all day reading the Life of David Cockburn's travels, and "The Jewish Spie" at night.

Jan. 21st. At home all day reading and writing. At night came Mr. Batty and John Oliver and paid me eighty two pounds and seven shillings.

Jan. 23rd. Rid to Fford. Dined with Mr. Bagshaw. We were treated with an Ananas, or Pine apple, of a most delicious taste and flavour, the growth of the High Peak, and ripe on the 23rd of January in an hard winter. (35.)

Feb. 23rd. At home all day reading and writing and correcting a volume of Mr. Ashe's sermons yt is intended for ye press.

(34). Charles VI., Emperor of Germany, son of Leopold I. and father of the celebrated Maria Theresa. The Empress Anne of Russia.

(35). The first pine-apples were cultivated in England by Sir Matthew Decker, at Richmond. It was still a rarity when Dr. Clegg tasted one.
" If the general or at least if the Judgment of the most numerous Part of Mankind who have tasted of this fruit may be relied upon, it deserves the Preference of all other fruits ; the agreeable variety and the delicate quick piquancy of its juice is justly esteemed to excel every other."—Hughes' Natural Hist. of Barbados, 1750.

March 13th. Had some disturbance with the Chelmorton people, teazing me for moneys which I had not for them.

1741. April 1st. A messenger came with a letter from Mr. Mills, desiring me to apply to Justice Bagshaw to sign a petition for reprieving and transporting a criminal condemned to die at Derby. I rid over to Tideswell and succeeded, and returned much fatigued.

April 3rd. Last night my man left a young heifer thro' carelessness in ye fields; she did not come with ye rest; he did not seek her nor mention her to us, and this morning she was found dead. Its a loss and a great disappointment, and it grieves me yt it was occasioned by carelessness, but such rebukes may be needful and useful.

June 22nd. (Dr. Clegg, with his daughters Sally and Betty, was very ill from this day for some weeks, a kind of malarial fever with ague which was very prevalent in the parish.)

July 14th. My dear daughter (Sally) is stil' alive but in as low a condition as it is possible for any one to be in and live, yet the plaister had raised a blister and made a great discharge, but stil' she continued insensible and unable to speak. About noon she was seized with a sort of universal convulsion that shook the bed. This was followed by strong pain, as we concluded from her groaning and mournful complaint; and about half an hour past two she departed this life, aged 23 years one month and 14 days. She died on the 16th day of her fever, which was of the nervous kind. She was the most pious and dutiful child I ever had, and this is the greatest breach that was ever made upon my earthly comforts. She was a most dutiful and affectionate daughter to me, of an excellent capacity and great ingenuity; but what was most valuable in her was her real piety. Her life was pure and unblemished, useful and exemplary, and her conversation both agreeable and instructive. She was exceeding willing to die, and told me she has no cloud, but peace within, and begged I would no longer pray for her life but resign her to God.

July 16. I am still taken up more than I could wish with cares about the funeral, but its what ye custom of the country renders necessary, and I would not willingly give any just occasion of offence. I hope God will not impute this care to me for sin.

July 30th. Went up to Chappel to hire men and horses for Mrs Gleg. Agreed with Chas. Shirt to carry them to York for four pounds and to bear his own charges both for men and horses.

Aug. 6th. After dinner went up to town. Had a tooth drawn by Edw. Bennet which had caused me a great deal of trouble for a considerable time. He did it well, but I lost a good deal of blood.

Sept. 7th.   There are many complaints of the scarcity of hay in the parts about, but I never knew a more plentiful year in this parish, nor more fine and seasonable weather for gathering in both the hay and the corn.

Sept. 17th.   This day ye Duke of Devonshire set out for Ireland.   (Having been appointed Lord Lieutenant.)

Sept. 22nd.   I have receivd a volume of Mr. Ashe's sermons which I lately fitted for ye press.   Its now well printed and I hope the book will be of good use.

Sept. 24th.   Came safe to Gainsborough.   There I found a good old acquaintance whom I had not seen in forty years before, that was Mr. Anthony Hadfield.   He had served apprenticeship to a merchant in Hull, had been 30 years and more in Africa, seven years ye British Consul at Tetuan, and is now returned to pass the remainder of his time in his native country; and great was our mutual rejoycing.

Sept. 28th.   (Still at Gainsborough.)   In the afternoon I went to see the Orrery and Similo, fine machines for showing ye situations and the motions of ye celestial bodies, according to both ye Ptolemaic and Copernican systems.   (36.)

Oct. 29th.   Received a parcel of books from London; " ye Philosophical Grammar," &c.

Nov. 2nd.   At home all day perusing some of my new books that afforded good entertainment.

Nov. 8th.   This night one David Taylor, a Methodist, began to preach amongst us.   He preached in ye street at Chappel-le-Frith, but some persons set ye bells a ringing, which gave him great disturbance, and highly provoked many.   (37.)

Nov. 14th.   Sent Mr. Goddard a cheese of value.   The

---

(36). The Orrery was called after Charles Boyle, Earl of Orrery, who was said to have invented it. It was a machine for illustrating and exploring the motions of the heavenly bodies. What was a Similo?

(37). This visit of David Taylor must have been in the earliest part of the Methodist revival. The knot of enthusiasts who began the revival at Oxford only removed to London in 1738; and Whitfield began his preaching after that Hegira. David Taylor, originally a servant of Lady Huntingdon, was one of Wesley's first preachers, but afterwards left the work. He raised up a number of Methodist Churches in Derbyshire and Yorkshire, but contracted an ill-judged marriage and "had fallen into German stillness." Some say he had been one of the servants of the Earl of Huntingdon; others say he had been a footman to Lady Margt. Hastings; and others that he had been butler to Lady Betty. Being converted under Ingham's preaching, and being a man of ability and of some education, the Countess of Huntingdon had sent him into the surrounding hamlets and villages to preach, and by degrees his labours were extended to various parts of Derbyshire, Cheshire, and Yorkshire. One of his converts was John Bennet, of Chinley, afterwards the husband of the well known Grace Murray. See Life of Wesley, by Tyerman.

Methodist has been preaching twice or 3 times a day all this week at Chinley End, or Heafield, or Marple, or elsewhere, and is attended by great numbers of people in all places. He seems a pious, zealous, well-meaning man, of great assurance, but little learning or knowledge.

Nov. 15th. Many came to hear David Taylor, who at noon preached on the Common near Gorsty Low to a great multitude. I scarce ever saw our Chappel so full as it was in the afternoon. God grant some good and lasting impressions may remain. I think it does not become us to give these Methodists any disturbance or opposition. Gamaliel's advice in such cases will always be found the best.

Nov. 23rd. Called on Mr. Tricket, just returned from Lincolnshire. He gave me an account of a barbarous murder, and a ruinous breach by Sir Brownlow Sherards going off into France for debt.

Nov. 25th. This was observed as a Day of Humiliation and very slightly by most about us.

Dec. 7th. Heard of the death of Col. Wm. Degge our landlord. (38.)

Dec. 20th. Had letters from Mr. Chandler and Mr. Rogerson acquainting me with the grant of an Exhibition from ye fund, for the education of my son Benjamin at ye Academy.

1741-2. Jan. 4th. David Taylor ye Methodist came amongst us again, and many flock to hear him. If any good be done I shall rejoice, and I ought to do so, by whatever person it is done.

Jan. 5th. We had most of our neighbours to supper. Had some discourse with them about David Taylor's doctrine, which I find leads to Antinomianism, which they are not sufficiently apprehensive of in its tendency. (39.)

Jan. 8th. I read lectures to Benjamin on his logick.

Jan. 11th. Reading lectures to Benjamin, and reading other books. I hear the Methodist has been preaching in Cheshire, and was admitted into the Pulpit of Smith, the Scotchman, in Stockport. Smith and he agree well I suppose in their notions.

Jan. 12th. At night I was invited by 2 messages to see and talk with ye Methodist, who preached today at Milton and was

(38). Col. Wm. Degge was owner of the Bowden Hall estate, which included Stodhart, where Dr. Clegg lived. He was the son of Simon Degge and great-grandson of Sir Simon Degge, Recorder of Derby and Judge of West Wales. Col. Wm. Degge died Nov. 23rd, 1741, in Dublin.

(39). Antinomianism is described in the dictionaries as the "Doctrine of Salvation by Grace alone, without works," held by the Calvinists.

invited to Job Bennets at night. I enquired after his authority to preach; he could not pretend to any but an inward motion of the Spirit. I then enquired what doctrines he preached, and found them Antinomian to the highest degree; he tells his hearers that they are all lost in Adam's sin, that they can do nothing at all towards their own recovery, nor need to do anything, Christ having done all. He makes no manner of account of repentance or holiness or obedience. He prayed to God that he might never have any holiness or righteousness of his own as long as he lives. I shewed him from Scripture and reason the necessity of holiness and virtue of obedience and goodness til' he was silenced, but he would not be convinced, and so I left him. I bless God that I was enabled to deal so plainly and faithfully with him, in ye presence of so many of his friends. Some were satisfied and returned me thanks, but some others flock after him stil' and I fear to their hurt.

Jan. 15th. Gave an account (at Chinley House) of my conference with ye Methodist. I find he has created very great uneasiness and disturbance in the minds of many. He goes to houses where he is never invited and tells the most serious and pious women they are whores, fornicators, adulteresses and murderers &c. Thus he talked to Sarah the wife of John Carrington, a woman of good sense and of an unblemished character, who was big with child and near her time. The shock it gave her and the fright it put her into went near to cause a miscarriage, which would have endangered her life. I earnestly pray that it may please God to preserve my people from infection, and to deliver them from this man.

Jan. 30th. (Mrs. Clegg died). This is the widest breach that was ever made upon me. The greatest loss I ever sustained. I am now deprived of a most pious, prudent, diligent, careful and affectionate companion.

Feb. 11th. At home all day. My good old friend Dr. Lee, Vicar of Halifax, called on me and sat with me an hour or two, to my great satisfaction.

1742. April 20th. Walked up to town to ye Parish Meeting about ye choice of Parish officers and spent some time with ye freeholders, and I hope it was not spent in vain.

April 26th. Great numbers of soldiers on the march were quartered abroad in ye parish, but none of them at my house. This morning most of them marched off. (40.)

May 12th. (Manchester.) I went with Mr. Shaw to the College, and after to see Mr. Berry's garden in Salford, in which

(40). England was at this time at war, and soldiers were being marched for embarcation to Germany, and possibly to take their share in the Battle of Dettingen.

I met with such a collection of Rare and Exotic plants and curious flowers as I had never seen before.

May 25th. At home reading Dr. Owen's "Natural History of Serpents," but very little to my advantage.

July 15th. This day the wife of John Bennet, brother of William Bennet's wife, of Chinley End, was interred at Chappel-en-le-Frith. Its said she had been vilely abused if not ravished by one Thomas Good, a butcher in Buxton, and that the bruises she received were ye occasion of her sickness and death. If this be true, it is a crime that deserves to be punished by ye Judge. Good Lord put a stop to ye progress of vice!

Aug. 11th. I read Mr. Balguy's Essay on Redemption and was very much pleased with it.

Sept. 17th. On Thursday I heard that Jos. Bott of Chelmorton was killed by a wain wheel going over his head. This is a sad disaster, a great loss to his family and to ye poor society at Chelmorton, for he was the most honest and active and publick-spirited person amongst them.

Oct. 15th. I received a seasonable supply from Dr. Wright, he sent me an order for receiving ten pounds. This is a remarkable token of divine favour and goodness.

Nov. 10th. It was ye Publick Ffast, and I preached from I. Tim. 2, 1 and 2, to a numerous congregation. The Ffast was generally strictly observed in this part.

Dec. 7th. I was at home all day reading some sermons preached by Mr. Whitfield in Scotland. I find he is running into ye Height of Antinomianism, and that is ye tendency of all the doctrine of the Methodists. May a stop be put to the spreading of those gross and dangerous errors and delusions.

Dec. 22nd. Ye ffatt swine was killed.

Dec. 27th. I was at home til' noon, and then walked down to see Peter Wood, who had been confined a great part of ye week before for another person's debt.

Dec. 28th. At Lydiat. I bought the grey mare for 7 guineas.

1742-3. Jan. 20th. I set out with my mare for Macclesfield, consulted with Mr. Heald, &c., about securing a considerable legacy left by Joseph Warren, of Macclesfield Forest, to ye Ministers of Buxton, Chelmorton, Hucklow, and Middleton.

Jan. 25th. I set out for home (from Buxton) leaving son Benjamin to bath in ye well, and drink the water this week, to cleanse him from ye itch and scorbutic humours.

Jan. 27th. I went up to Chappel fair and bought a pair of bullocks.

Jan. 30th. I preached twice from Matt. 7, 2. I used ye best endeavours I could to prevent or cure delusions by the Methodists, but I think what I said was ill taken by many of them. At night son Benjamin (who should have set out for Ffindern next day) appeared extremely uneasy to return, pretending he was not cured of ye itch, and used language yt filled me with great uneasiness all ye night. May God make him more humble, meek and dutiful. I determined to keep him another week and try other remedies.

Febry. 13th. Robert Oliver brought me news of the death of Mr. Smalley, the Dissenting Minister at Chesterfield. He was a man much beloved for his pleasant conversation, of a good life, but no admired preacher.

Febry. 19th. In the evening Mr. Roger Evans came to us from Manchester. He is absconding from his creditors, and begged to stay til' he could agree with his creditors.

March 19th. I was at home revising and preparing sermons for the Lords Day. By the frequent disorders in my head and eyes I am often disabled from preparing new discourses, and am necessitated instead of that to review and correct some that were delivered some years since, which I hope may be as beneficial as if they were new.

1743. March 26th. Mr. Roger Evans left us this afternoon and set out for Manchester, his discharge being signed. He has been with us on free cost just 5 weeks.

March 31st. Went to Chappel, was called to Mr. Bardsley ye Clergyman, and gave him the best advice I could. (41).

April 16th. I took of squills and garlick infused in vinegar with Honey, and dissolved in it Gum Ammoniacum and Balsam of Tolu, and now and then I took spermaceti dissolved in hott broth (for Asthma).

April 26th. At home all day reading and writing about the preachings of the Methodists. I hear of several about, and some of my congregation are setting up to preach, to spread Antinomianism.

May 24th. I set out with my son and daughter for ye double Lecture at Stoney Middleton. Called at Tideswell to

(41). Mr. Benjamin Bardsley was Vicar of Chapel-en-le-Frith from 1727 to 1747. In 1747, at the death of Mr. Bardsley, the Dean and Chapter of Lichfield presented to Chapel-en-le-Frith, but the parishioners resisted, and eventually the advowson was again vested in the freeholders, then twenty-seven in number.

acquaint Mr. Kelsal with a letter from Mr. Mottershead and Justice Duckinfield, acquainting me that a woman had sworn before the Justice that Mr. Kelsal had a carnal knowledge of her, and that she was 6 months gone with child by him. This gave me great concern. He solemnly declared himself innocent of the fact he is charged with.

June 16th. I was at home til' afternoon, had some conversation with John Bennet, the Methodist, and delivered him a paper of my sentiments on his preaching. I read over Mr. Wesley's defence which he left with me. (42.)

June 17th. Walked to Malcoffe to baptize a child of Thomas Barber called Ellen. There was a great deal of company and I fear of excess. I wish we might have no more of such Christenings or Meetings. I think proper endeavours should be used that such customs should be broken and laid aside.

June 23rd. Went to Chappel. Had some debate with one of the Methodists which warmed me a little too much.

July 26th. In the morning I had the news from son Joseph of the Battle betwixt the English and the Ffrench in Germany, and our victory; which gave me great pleasure. (43.)

Aug. 31st. I received yesterday a large parcel of Bibles and Testaments to be given to the poor.

Sept. 14th. I sent some Bibles and Testaments to be disposed of amongst poor miners and others by Mr. Hadfield of Tideswell. I had sent some before to Mr. Fletcher at Eyam, to J. Soresby of Hucklow, and Mr. Harrison of Buxton. God grant that they may be well used, and help to promote useful knowledge.

Sept. 18th. Was much dejected under apprehensions of Divisions likely to be made amongst us by ye proceedings of ye Methodists.

Oct. 4th. (At Gainsborough.) I went with Mr. Woodhouse to a Lecture on Experimental Philosophy by one Mr. Miden or Mithin. It was on the influence of air and water in vegetation.

(42). John Bennet was born at Chinley in Derbyshire. He received a good education, and was always fond of books. At the age of 17 he was placed at Dr. Latham's well-known Academy at Findern, near Derby, with a view of studying for the Christian ministry. Before long, however, he engaged himself as clerk to a magistrate, and at 22 years of age embarked in the business of a carrier between Sheffield and Macclesfield, employing a number of horses for carrying 'goods across mountains over which carts or waggons had never passed. In 1739 he went to Sheffield Races, heard David Taylor preach, sold his racehorses, brought Taylor into Derbyshire, and was converted. He soon relinquished all secular pursuits, and began to preach himself on Oct. 3rd, 1749.—See Life of Wesley, by Tyerman.

(43). This must refer to the Battle of Dettingen, which was fought June 27th, 1743.

Several experiments were tried with the air pump to show the manner of respiration, &c.

Oct. 18th. Sent the first making of corn to the mill. I had a greater produce than ever before, blessed be God.

Oct. 20th. My birthday. At night my neighbours came in and I gave them a small entertainment and we were, I hope innocently, merry.

Oct. 31st. At home all day reading Millar's History and Butler's Analogy.

Nov. 10th. I had two letters from son James, one to acquaint me yt son Waterhouse's horse was stolen on ye 5th November. I got it cried at the Cross, and Mr. Rogerson is writing and sending abroad advertisements around us about it. (43A.)

Nov. 12th. Sent my man to Justice Chetham for a warrant to apprehend Barrow on suspicion of his having stole son Waterhouse's horse, and he was apprehended and secured.

Dec. 6th. Mr. Berry brought and fitted me up an Horizontal weather glass, for which I paid him half a guinea.

Dec. 15th. Spent some time at an auction of books and maps, &c., at ye Royal Oak.

1743-4. Jan. 4th. We were all invited to dine at Fford, where there was a great deal of company, but I had little satisfaction in it, not having an opportunity nor an heart to do any good.

Jan. 6th. We had some neighbours to supper this night, and it kept us up too late. For that and other reasons I determine if it pleased God to spare me another year, not to have them to supper but to dinner.

Jan. 12th. Walked up to Chappel on Parish business and writ an agreement that was made with John Fox for maintaining all ye poor for one year at 12d. per head. It was signed by the Parishioners that were present.

Febry. 7th. On the way (to Shireoaks) was an ugly yate which I could not open sufficiently for ye mare to pass, but she rushed through it, and my leg was catched in it, and I was plucked off. I fell with my head on an ice, and was wounded and lost some blood, and had a hurt on my leg.

Febry. 26th. We hear the Ffrench are attempting to invade

(43A). The old market cross, still standing in Chapel-en-le-Frith.

us. About 20 of their men of war are now in the Channel, with ye Pretender's eldest son. (44.)

March 21st. We hear that Admiral Matthews has defeated ye Spanish fleet, and that the Ffrench are retired from Dunkirk, after suffering great loss from stormy weather. Blessed be God who fighteth for us and blasteth ye designs of our Enemies! (45.)

1744. April 3rd. I received from son Joseph the King's Declaration of War against the Ffrench. May God prosper him in it, and give success to our forces by sea and land.

April 18th. They are pressing men for the war.

May 8th. (At Manchester.) Dined with 39 Ministers at the cost of Mr. Butterworth. (45A.)

May 9th. I walked to see a fine garden in Salford, then to ye Library in ye College. (Chetham College.)

May 24th. (At Macclesfield.) I found an unhappy difference betwixt ye Trustees of ye Meeting Place at Macclesfield and Mr. Acton. I laboured to heal it but could not prevail. Pride and self love are too prevalent in us.

June 4th. Had some workmen to make up our bath, who after fished ye brook, and several came to see the diversion.

June 11th. I rid over into Barmoor with Mr. Slack and bought a young horse, cost 5£ 8s. 6d., and brought it with us.

June 14th. Mr. Thos. Higginbottom and his brother came to me to propose a marriage betwixt yr nephew Thos. Middleton and daughter Betty.

July 25th. Walked up to Chappel to peruse a settlement deed, on behalfe of my daughter, who intends shortly to be married to Thos. Middleton, grandson to Mr. Robt. Middleton my old friend.

July 27th. My daughter was married this morning by Mr. Bardsley at Chappel-en-le-Frith. We all dined at Thos. Middletons, and I returned with my sons about the middle of the afternoon. I am now left in solitary state. Son Benjamin sets out

---

(44). Charles Edward the Pretender was placed in 1744 by the French Government at the head of a formidable armament, but his plan of a descent upon Scotland was frustrated by a violent storm which wrecked his fleet.

(45). Febry. 22nd, 1744, N.S. Admiral Matthews attacked the Spanish fleet off Toulon and defeated them.

(45A). Thomas Butterworth was a trustee of Corn Street Chapel, Manchester. He married a daughter of Sir Robert Dukinfield, and died 15th December, 1745, aged 62.

for the Academy at Kendal, and then I shall have no child with me. I am therefore advised by my children and friends to look out for a suitable companion.

July 28th. This morning ye young pair breakfasted with us and some other young persons, and I endeavoured humbly to recommend them to Divine favour by earnest prayer.

Aug. 16th. Walked up to Chappel, met Mr. Thomas Kyrke and came to a conclusion about marrying. I had been in great perplexity about it, but now resolved to follow ye conduct of Providence and cast all my care upon the ever blessed God.

Aug. 17th. I was much indisposed, and afflicted with what we call yé Hypocondriac passion.

Aug. 22nd. I set out with my friends to Disley and there was married by Mr. Robinson of Macclesfield to Mrs. Eyre. Mr. Culcheth and Mr. Jones were with us, and several other friends. (46.)

Aug. 23rd. I find myselfe now much better both in body and mind; calm, cheerful, composed and easy.

Aug. 24th. Mr. Fletcher came to see us and dined with us; so did son and daughter Middleton. They then set out for the Races at Tideswell, and I sent my man with them. It was late before they returned.

Sept. 13th. Stil' very heavy rain, and the greatest flood I have known in 30 years past. We were detained at home; none could come to us without danger til' far after noon.

Sept. 18th. Last night I was in great danger of being suffocated and burned in bed. Ye candle fell on the bed when I was drop'd asleep, and set fire to the bed. Blessed be God for this remarkable deliverance!

Oct. 7th. Afternoon my wife and her daughter were at Church.

1744-5. Jan. 17th. We were invited to dine at Fford, and I took my wife with me and Ms. Eyre. The latter stayed there all night and the night after. I returned after dinner with my wife, and my man having got too much drink fell from ye mare and was in great danger of losing his life.

Jan. 21st. I heard of the death of Robt. Bennet, ye son of Christopher Bennet of Whitehough head. He had, alas, been a

---

(46). Mrs. Eyre was Sarah, sister of the Rev. John Jones, of Marple (a special friend of Dr. Clegg), and widow of Thos. Eyre, Esq., of Hathersage and Stockport, who died in 1732. Her daughter Anne was the Miss Eyre so frequently mentioned in the Diary, and Gillingham Eyre (the Gilly of the Diary) was the child of her son, the Rev. Thomas Eyre, of Stockport.

stubborn perverse youth, and in that temper he died, ordering himselfe to be buried at ye end of his house, in his cloaths, and so we hear he was buried.

Jan. 26th. My dear hears bad news from abroad. A ship is taken by ye Ffrench which had 700 pounds worth of silk on board, pertaining to the mill at Stockport. A 12th of the loss lies upon her.

Febry. 11th. The Reverend Mr. Ferdinando Shaw, Minister at Derby, departed this life Jan. 27th, about the 73rd year of his life. I who when I came into this County was one of the youngest, am now the oldest minister in the County.

1745. May 13th. I set out for Roachdale. On the road my mare stumbled and came down, and cast me over her head, down a very steep hill. I fell on my head and was in great danger of losing my life, but God mercifully preserved it.

June 7th. I read several things of Mr. Wesley's and was glad to find him so thoroughly convinced of the falsehood and bad tendency of Antinomianism that prevails so much amongst ye Methodists.

July 1st. Was called to see Mrs. Worthington, in an Hysterick disorder, occasioned by the death of her child and a scandal cast on her husband.

Aug. 18th. Last night there was a rush-bearing at Chappel-en-le-Frith, and a daughter of John Pickford of the Royal Oak in Chappel and his man servant had each an arm broken by falls. (47.)

Aug. 19th. Edw. Bennet came from Chelmorton with some unreasonable demands, and I gave too much way to passion. May God forgive it!

Sept. 3rd. I rid over to Buxton to assist in settling accounts with Edw. Bennet of Chelmorton about ye Meeting Place there. Met with Capt. Harrison, Captain of ye ship Tiger. My man was sadly disordered by strong drink, to my great vexation and griefe.

Sept. 5th. Ms. Eyre and Ms. Hall went to Tideswell Races, but returned in good time and had no misfortune.

Sept. 24th. Today we hear the Scotch Rebels are in posses-

---

(47). In the olden days the church was unwarmed, so it was strewn with rushes to protect the feet of the worshippers. These rushes were renewed only once a year, when the parishioners turned out to cut rushes, which were brought home in carts decorated with flags and flowers and preceded by music. The day was observed as a holiday, and generally finished with much drunkenness and debauchery

sion of the City of Edinburgh, and for advancing towards England speedily.

Sept. 26th. I had an account from my son James of the defeat of the Kings forces by ye Rebels in Scotland, and sent ye account to Fford.

Sept. 27th. All about us in great consternation, under apprehensions of ye progress of the Rebellion. Our Gentlemen set out to meet ye Duke of Devonshire at Derby, to concert measures for raising forces for the defence of the Nation.

Oct. 2nd. We hear the Highland Rebels are returned back to Edinburgh, endeavouring to have that Castle surrendered to them. This gives more time to the Government for raising forces.

Oct. 4th. I was called to Mr. Fletcher of Eyam, dangerously ill, either through the carelessness or ignorance of an Apothecary in making him up a dose of Physick that went near to kill him.

Oct. 6th. I was much indisposed by ye Hypocondriac wind all the night before, and all this day.

Oct. 8th. This morning I had a letter to acquaint me with the death of my dear friend and brother Mr. Edmund Fletcher. I writ to Mr. Kelsal to enquire into ye preparation of ye potion for Mr. Fletcher.

Oct. 10th. I set out for Eyam to the funeral of Mr. Fletcher. There I met with a letter from Thos. Beech who made up ye Physick for Mr. Fletcher, declaring the prescription was very safe and rightly prepared, but he did not say he made it up, or saw it made up, which makes me stil' suspect there was a fatal error, and that 2 scruples of ye Emetic Salt of Tartar were put in, instead of yt quantity of ye plain Salt of Tartar, which was ordered.

Oct. 27th. I preached a funeral sermon for Mr. Fletcher to a numerous assembly, more than ye place could hold. I was about three hours and three quarters in ye pulpit, preaching only once, but at night was exceedingly spent.

Nov. 9th. Had a letter from son James with advice that the Rebels were advancing towards England, but it was not known whether they would come by Carlisle or ye Newcastle road.

Nov. 13th. We had advice that the people in Manchester are in great confusion, many of them removing their best effects.

Nov. 14th. We hear ye Rebels have laid seige to Carlisle.

Nov. 17th. We hear Carlisle surrendered on Fryday last, but the Castle stil' held out against ye Rebels.

Nov. 18th. I was reading Mr. Taylor on the Epistle to the Romans, a good performance in my Judgment, but I can't yet entirely come into his sentiments on all particulars.

Nov. 19th. Writing letters to Mr. Harrison and Mr. Chandler on behalfe of Mr. Bardsley's son, to procure him a Studentship at Christ Church College in Oxford.

Nov. 25th. We hear ye Rebels are advancing fast towards Manchester, and the people are removing and concealing their best effects.

Nov. 26th. Was called up to Chappel to dine with Mr. Butterworth and two of Mr. Bailey's sons and their wives, who are flying for safety to Sheffield. At night I sent away my wife's cloaths and Linen and some writings to be concealed awhile.

Nov. 27th. We hear some of ye Rebels are come to Manchester. Our town is full of Refugees.

Nov. 28th. Walked to Chappell to hear tidings and to visit my friends. All the news is discouraging; Stockport bridge is broken down, but we know not which way the Rebels intend to go from Manchester.

Nov. 29th. I walked up to town to hear tidings and see my friends; all are full of fears.

Nov. 30th. I spent some time with Justice Duckinfield. Sent two men to assist in making Trenches to obstruct the roads about Waley, but in my thought it could not answer any good purpose, but was very bad for travellers. (48.)

Dec. 1st. The Rebels left Manchester in ye morning and entered Macclesfield soon after noon and lodged there that night. I preached twice and, blessed be God, was quite free from distracting fears. Mrs. Duckingfield and her daughter came to lodge with us this night.

Dec. 2nd. The Rebels rested all day in Macclesfield, but soon had eaten up all their provisions, and made filthy and ruinous work in their houses. (49.)

---

(48). Whaley is a small village three miles from Chapel-en-le-Frith where a bridge crosses the river Goyt.

(49). "The Rebels asked for Sir Peter Davenports house whether he was in Town or not, and being answered not, they gave him a curse and soon after rode to his house, and after viewing it inside and out marked the door with the word 'Prince.' The Prince was in Highland Dress with a blue waistcoat braided with silver, and had on a blue Highland cap. He is a very handsome person of a man, rather tall, exactly proportioned and walks very well, but his face is not marked with the small-pox."
"I stepped over to a poor neighbour's house who had 50 common men quartered on him to see how they lay. The house floor was covered with

Dec. 3rd.   The Rebels left Macclesfield and took the road to Congleton, Leek and Ashbourne.

Dec. 4th.   Very early I sent my man to Derby with letters for son Ben., but he could not meet with him.   He left the letters and made haste out, and saw the Rebels marching very near to Derby as he came, and his mare narrowly escaped being pressed for the use of ye Rebels.   He came back in good time at night, having travelled about 54 miles that day.

Dec. 5th.   We heard all the Rebels were in Derby.   I set out with Mrs. Duckinfield to conduct them towards home.   We dined at Waley and there parted.   (50.)

Dec. 6th.   We hear ye Rebels apprehending ye King's forces to be near them returned in haste from Derby towards Ashbourne.

Dec. 7th.   A rumour prevailed that ye Rebels were just coming upon us, which occasioned great confusion, but they were

straw, and men, women, and children lay promiscuously together like a kennel of hounds and some of them even stark naked."

"I had 20 common men and 3 officers and 6 horses quartered on me. These officers are scrubby fellows and behave rudely.   One of them broke me a good looking glass, and the common men would have plundered me had they not been restrained.   Those townsmen who had locked their doors, and the houses of others who were not able to guard their effects were plundered, and many others were robbed of what money, bedding and cloathes they had, and nothing escaped that was portable and could be of any use to them. It appears that the officers had very little command over the men who pilfered and plundered all the way.   The officers for the most part behaved pretty well, but the common men like devils.   They not only lived upon free quarters in every house but plundered people of their money, bedding, cloathes and any thing they could carry away.   Their habits were filthy to a degree, fouling the houses and using the streets as in Edinburgh."

Letters of Mr. John Stafford, an attorney in Macclesfield, in Earwaker's East Cheshire.

(50). The Rebels were quartered in Derby.   The Prince at Lord Exeter's house and the officers in other houses.   Many common or ordinary houses had 40 or 50 men each and some gentlemen near an 100.   After supper being weary with their long march they went to rest, many upon straw and others in beds.   They were very alert the next day running about from one shop to another to buy or rather steal tradesmen's goods, Gloves, buckles, powder flasks, buttons, handkerchiefs, shoes, &c., and the town being filled with them looked like a Highland fair.   Nothing was more common for them if they liked a persons shoes better than their own to demand them off their feet and not give them anything.   The longer they stayed the more insolent and outrageous they grew, demanding everything by threats, drawn swords and pistolls clapped to the breast of many persons not only by common men but their officers.   They broke open closets, chests, boxes and took away all guns, pistols, swords and other arms; pilfered and stole linens, stockings, shoes and everything they could find.   In fact they committed all manner of outrages."—Contemporary M.S. quoted in Glover's Derbyshire.

At Leek.   "Our Meeting-house they broak open in the night and turned it into a stable, throwing the seats on an heap.   The Meeting House Chamber a kind of kitchen for dressing their meat, and filthy work was made in it, the scent continued for 2 weeks.   In the Chamber they broke open 2 chests to search for money.   The poor suffered extremely not only by robbing but the expense in entertaining such great numbers.   Those who left their houses were broak open and stript.   Carried off cheese and almost every horse."

Letters supposed to be by Mr. Joshua Toft.   See Sleigh's Hist. of Leek.

only advancing towards Macclesfield. Son Middleton was there on my mare but made haste out of town.

Dec. 8th. The whole army of ye Rebels was in Macclesfield this morning, but presently set off for Stockport.

Dec. 9th. We hear they have all left Stockport.

Dec. 10th. Ye Rebels have all returned to Manchester. They took several persons with them from Stockport. Blessed be God, ye silk mill is safe.

Dec. 11th. We hear some of ye King's forces, with ye Duke of Cumberland, are now in Macclesfield. I sent my man to Stockport for intelligence.

Dec. 12th. The last of ye Rebels left Manchester on Tuesday and carried off at this time 2,500 pounds in cash.

Dec. 13th. Son Middleton set out on my mare for Manchester. We had advice that ye Duke's forces were in pursuit of ye Rebels, and at Preston, not far behind them. Ye General Huske was got before them.

Dec. 15th. At night son Middleton returned, but brought us no intelligence, only that my sons in Manchester suffered no loss by ye Rebels but in their meat and drink.

Dec. 20th. Had advice from my son that ye Duke had cut off 100 of ye rear of ye Rebels, but yt ye body of them were got to Carlisle.

Dec. 22nd. I found I could not officiate (from pain and hoarseness) in the afternoon, so I ordered all my family to go to Church excepting Gilly and my son's child.

Dec. 27th. The day was very cold and stormy, and I continued at home all day. This week I sent away 2 potts of butter for son Joseph to London. A very mortal disease prevails among the cattle about London, and very few dare eat any Beefe or butter made there. We have advice that the French are about to land 15 or 20,000 men in England. May ye Almighty God in mercy appear for our defence.

Dec. 29th. We hear most of ye Rebels are got into Scotland with the wealth and plunder they have carried out of England, to our loss and shame.

Dec. 30th. We hear ye Duke of Cumberland is beseiging Carlisle.

Dec. 31st. With regard to public affairs this year has been unhappy. Our forces and those of ye Allies of Brittain have been worsted in Flanders, in Germany, in Italy and in Scotland, and ye Rebels from thence have ravaged and plundered six counties in England and 12 large towns.

1745-6. Jan. 1st. We have an account in ye publick papers of a peace concluded betwixt the K. of Prussia and Poland and the Queen of Hungary. Ye rumour of an invasion from France begins to abate, which may be owing in part to ye success Admiral Townsend has had in destroying their Martinico Fleet.

Jan. 4th. I had advice from Mr. Bayley of Manchester that Carlisle was surrendered by the Rebels, and all of them that were in it, some say 400 others 700, made prisoners at Discretion.

Jan. 9th. I visited Geo. Bramhall whose colick ends in the Iliac passion and I doubt will take him off. This day I sent my son John in Manchester an horse load of provisions, meal, bacon, cheese, and butter, towards making up the loss he sustained by the devouring Rebels.

Jan. 27th. I had advice from Manchester that there has been another battle with ye Rebels in ye North, in which they have lost more men, but one wing of our army has suffered pretty much. (51.)

Febry. 2nd. Last week I had a present of a book from Mr. John Wesley, which he lately published, called " A further Appeal to men of Reason and Religion." I read it with pleasure and I hope with profit. (52.)

Febry. 8th. The Bells were rung at Chappel-en-le-Frith from 7 in the morning til' 4 afternoon on advice of ye Duke's raising ye seige of Stirling Castle.

Febry. 15th. Had an express from Manchester with accounts of the Duke of Cumberland's success in Scotland. Ye Rebels seem to be breaking and despersing.

March 2nd. In the morning I was in great perplexity about my spiritual state, but after earnest prayer it pleased God to give me some ease.

1746. March 28th. I settled accounts with my wife, and

(51). Probably the Battle of Falkirk.

(52). John Wesley paid more than one visit to Chapel-en-le-Frith. At a later date, viz.: March, 1785, he came to the parish, where a large number had been converted but needed discipline. In a letter about that date he writes of them :—" Frequently 3 or 4, 10 or 12 pray aloud all together. Some of them perhaps many scream all together as loud as they possibly can. Some use improper yea indecent expressions in prayers. Several drop down as dead, and are as stiff as a corpse, but in a while they start up and cry Glory ! Glory ! perhaps 20 times together. Just so do the French people, and very lately the jumpers in Wales and bring the real work into contempt. Yet whenever we reprove them, it should be in the most mild and gentle manner possible."

she paid me what I had laid out for her, and for one years board for her daughter and grandson. In all it amounted to 34£ 18s.

March 29th. On Thursday last we felled ye great tree near the house, and my man narrowly escaped being killed.

April 29th. We have good news from Scotland and from Italy too.

April 30th. Great rejoycings for the Duke's Victory (at Culloden).

June 4th. This day a messenger came to acquaint me with the death of my Ffather-in-law Mr. Joseph Champion of Edale. He was in the 94th year of his age or the 95th. His widow is now in the 88th or 89th. They had been married about 68 years and lived in love and peace all along.

June 24th. We hear of a bloody murder committed by one of the Methodists near Cheadle in Cheshire. A weaver there has in an enthusiastic frenzy cut ye throat of an apprentice he had, about 13 years old. May the merciful God prevent the like amongst us.

July 9th. My son and Ms Eyre set out for Disley to meet some friends from Prestbury, and to see the house at Lime. (53.) They were out too late. When they returned they brought me the shocking and afflicting tidings that my friend Mr. Geo. Heald of Macclesfield had hanged himself in great distraction of mind, which had gradually been growing on him for several weeks, occasioned by the bad conduct of his only son. This was a very great and a sad surprise to me, that a man of so much piety, knowledge and good sense should be hurried by passion to the commision of such an horrible and unnatural fact.

Aug. 21st. We hear of a signal victory gained by ye Austrians over ye French and Spaniards. (54.)

Oct. 4th. Called to a child of Thos. Barber of Malcoffe. In alighting at that door my feet shot under ye mare's belly and I was down on my back, the mare set one foot on my breast but so gently I had little harm.

Oct. 9th. This was the Thanksgiving Day for ye Victory over ye Rebels.

Oct. 17th. This night a man driving a team near Lightbirch was killed by a squeaze betwixt ye cart and a yate stoop. We passed by him a little before.

(53). Lyme Hall, a seat of the ancient family of Legh, of Cheshire, now represented by Lord Newton.

(54). Possibly the Battle of Placentia.

L

Nov. 2nd. This day we hear that my dear friend Capt. Bagshaw's left leg is taken off by a cannon ball, at ye seige of Port L'Orient in France, but its hoped he is almost out of danger. (55.)

Nov. 14th. Our servant Ruth left us, a very stubborn young woman. I fear she had got no good in our family.

1746-7. Jan. 29th. A fair in Chappel, but few cattle there, an Order in Council prohibiting the driving of lean cattle lest the infection should spread.

Febry. 14th. Ye moon was totally eclipsed.

1747. April 2nd. (At Manchester.) We saw the Electrical Experiments.

April 26th. Last night some wagon loads of convicted Rebels were brought to Chappel on yr way to Leverpool to be transported. Great numbers are running to see those poor wretches.

May 28th. We have had tidings of good success at sea in taking six French men of war and their East India Fleet, and now they are brought into Harbour. (56.)

June 15th. (Monday.) I preached at Ashford, and after dinner set out with Ms Eyre and others to see Chatsworth, and returned to Ashford.

June 16th. We spent ye morning in fishing in ye river.

July 3rd. We had news of a battle in Flanders in which I fear our forces were worsted, but ye French lost more men and have no reason for boasting, we hear. 32 of their Domingo Fleet are brought in. (57.)

July 12th. Was what they call the Wakes at Chappel. (58.)

Sept. 1st. I sold my two fat cows to a butcher of Ashton for 6

---

(55). Troops were sent from England under General St. Clair to surprise Port L'Orient and destroy the ships and stores of the French East India Company, but the expedition was a failure, and the only result attained was the plunder and burning of a few defenceless villages.

(56). Hawke's Victory off Belleisle.

(57). Defeat of the Duke of Cumberland by Marshal Saxe, at Lauffeld.

(58). The great festival in the parish is called the wakes. The Church is dedicated to S. Thomas a Becket, whose day is the 7th July. So the wakes are always held on the Sunday following that date and succeeding days. Masquerading, racing, bear-baiting, preceded by a cattle fair, were the chief amusements in olden times. Now the festival is celebrated by steam hurdy-gurdys and merry-go-rounds and the usual concomitants of a fair.

pounds 15 shillings. Our second crop of clover grass was well got in yesterday.

Sept. 15th. We hear Bergen op Zoom is taken by the French; treacherously betrayed.

Sept. 18th. A letter came by ye Post from London, but Shepley refused to deliver it out of the office unless I will pay an half penny more than the Law requires, which I am not willing to do; he has abused us other ways, and I'm determined to seek for satisfaction.

Oct. 1st. There was a fair at Chappel but few cattle came to it. We hear ye mortal disease prevails very much in ye neighbouring counties and is entered into this.

Oct. 11th. Much disturbed in mind on account of a dispute with the postmaster at Chappel, who has treated me with great injustice and persists in it. I have complained of it to Justice Chetham, but instead of procuring justice, he has sent me an order to appear before him and prove what I have alleged on Tuesday next.

Oct. 13th. I rid over to Mellor and took Ms. Eyre and son Middleton, Ms. Hall and Mr. Ed. Bennet with me to prove ye facts charged on Shepley, but the Justice was not at home. Shepley had appointed the day without the Justice's knowledge, or any order from him.

Dec. 1st. Such a quantity of snow fell in the night past, and the wind drove it into such heaps as have filled up the lanes and rendered them impassible for man or beast. Blessed be God, we are well furnished with fuel.

Dec. 3rd. The weather continued as severe as ever. We hear a poor woman is starved to death and two men, ye men on an hill called Stone Edge, on the road to Sheffield, but I don't hear that any near us are lost.

Dec. 22nd. I was at home all day reading Mr. Wests book on the Resurrection of Jesus Christ.

1747-8. Jan. 8th. We had several of our neighbours to supper, but they parted in pretty good time and without any disorder.

Jan. 12th. This day Mr. Bardsley is to be interred at ye Church. This is the 3rd Clergyman that has died in my time.

Jan. 21st. I read over the Life of Bishop Grindal.

Febry. 2nd. Went to Ford, dined there with Mr. Seward the Rector of Eyam. (59.)

1748. June 11th. Young Mr. Byrom has at length got the Curacy of Chappel-en-le-Frith, and there has been ringing and great rejoicing for it.

June 23rd. Two taylors came from Prestbury to make me cloaths.

June 26th. In the evening after I returned home, about ten minutes past five, we felt a shock of Earthquake which startled us all and sadly terrified some young women with us. It shook the whole town of Chappel-en-le-Frith and all the ground about it, and was perceived at Wash and Milton, and all about a mile about us, but blessed be God no hurt was done. The two days past had been excessively hott.

July 14th. This day the sun was nearly totally eclipsed, but we had no great darkness, but a great and heavy shower of rain.

July 23rd. We had a violent storm of loud thunder, and lightning, attended and followed by ye most heavy rain I ever saw, for about two hours, which raised the waters to a vast height and in a little it did incredible damage.

Augst. 4th. Carried my wife to Chinley Head, only for a ride out, for we never alighted, but we narrowly escaped a fall from the mare. Something in ye saddle or pilion hurt her and she kicked ; my wife came off, but blessed be God had no hurt.

Augst. 18th. (At Manchester.) Was at morning prayer at ye Old Church.

Nov. 24th. (Mrs. Clegg died after five days' illness.) Thus the wise, the just and good God has seen fitt to deprive me of an excellent woman, a pleasant companion, and a most affectionate wife, and I am left in my advanced age in a solitary state.

Dec. 6th. My heart is heavy, and at times full of sorrow, for the great loss of my dear wife. I would submit, but cannot

(59). The Rev Thomas Seward was Rector of Eyam for many years, and died at an advanced age in 1790. He published an edition of Beaumont and Fletcher, and his verses are preserved in Dodsley's Collection. His daughter Anna Seward, the poetess, was born at Eyam. She was a precocious child who at three years of age could lisp the allegro of Milton. She wrote a life of Darwin and many poems, which, with her letters, was published and edited by Sir Walter Scott. Peter Cunningham, the poet, was Seward's curate.

Mr. Seward was a friend of Dr. Johnson, and is mentioned in Boswell's Life several times.

yet conquer griefe. When I recollect ye agreeableness of her person, the beauties that even in her advanced age adorned her body and mind; when I reflect on her good sense and judgment, her great prudence and discretion, ye cheerfulness of her temper and conversation, and her most affectionate concern for my health and ease and satisfaction, it fills me with sorrow that I cannot express, and scarce know how to bear.

Dec. 26th. We hear the Marquess of Hartington has a son born.

Dec. 31st. Upon a review of the year I find that we have not had any great disaster in the warr by land, but signal successes at sea, and a peace is concluded. (60.)

1748-9. Jan. 8th. We had a flood in the morning. Son Benjamin preached. I hear the Methodists were offended with his discourse, he insisted so much on the necessity of a good life in order to Salvation by Christ.

Jan. 24th. I was at home all day, reviewing and destroying many hundreds of letters. Many of them it would not have been proper for any other person to have seen after my decease.

Febry. 13th. I set out with Ms. Eyre for Macclesfield; got there in good time. The peace was proclaimed there about 5 in the afternoon.

Febry. 25th. My good old black mare is now in great danger, being fallen down in the stable, and I fear will rise no more.

March 7th. Some harsh language that passed between me and Ms. Eyre gave me great uneasiness after.

March 8th. Ms. Eyre left us in displeasure, to my griefe, and went to Mrs. Bockins.

1749. March 27th. I set out with son John for Macclesfield on Ms. Eyre's account. It was thought necessary that I should take Letters of Administration from yt called the Spiritual Court, to enable me to dispose of the estate and effects of my late dear wife, but I soon convinced ye parties concerned that I had no occasion for them, but that all ye effects were absolutely my own, and that I could without leave of ye Court dispose of them as I thought fitt.

April 13th. The Court Leet was held at Chappel and I went up and spent some time with the Steward and several neigh-

(60). Peace of Aixe-la-Chapelle.

bours. Ten levies were assessed to defend our Liberties with regard to the grinding of our corn. (61.)

April 29th. I took a ride to Disley and met there with Mr. Cooper the Attorney, Mr. Jones, Mr. Bancroft and Ms. Anne Eyre, and I sealed a deed by which I made over the Estate of my late dear wife to her children and descendants. It is a great satisfaction to me that I have done it. I am now eased of a burden.

March 26th. Son Benjamin tells me he is called to be Minister at Mansfield, and has accepted the call. He says he must in a short time have been obliged to quit Pontefract through the failure of the salary, occasioned by the destructive disease amongst the cattle in those parts. What a seasonable provision has God made for him. For ever blessed be God for all his goodness to me and mine.

June 3rd. We have for some days past had so much frost and snow as I never knew before at this time of ye year.

July 19th. It gives me some trouble that I did not visit my aged friends when I might have done it; now I am disabled to do it, my good old mare being fallen lame, and I am confined at home. May I make some good use of my time there.

Augst. 2nd. My son James came to us, and I called son John to account for his undutiful behaviour to me, and laid his conduct before his brothers and sisters, which raised in them great indignation and griefe; but he was obstinate, and filled with rage, without relenting. They all agreed he and his family should be sent back to Manchester as soon as possible.

Augst. 7th. My son John took out and sent away all his goods. I was all ye day almost at son Middletons, whither John came up to me at night to beg forgiveness for his behaviour, but confessed not any faults in particular, nor seemed sufficiently humble. I said a great deal to him, but with too much passion. May God forgive me what I said amiss.

Nov. 24th. In ye morning our neighbour Thos. Bramhall's wife in travail was said to be in great danger, and all about her were greatly discouraged. I went up to my closet and prayed earnestly to God for her deliverance, and presently after she was safely delivered.

(61). "In the Civil Government of the Village there is the Lord of the soyl who from the Crown immediately or mediately holds Dominium Soli, and is said to have in him the Royalty, as if he were a little King, and hath a kind of jurisdiction over the inhabitants of the Village, hath his Court Leet or Court Baron to which they owe suit and service and where may be tried smaller matters happening within the Mannour; Escheats upon Felonies or other accidents, custody of Infants and Lunaticks, power of passing Estates and admitting Tenants, Reliefs, Heriots, Hunting, Hawking, Fishing, &c., &c."—Chamberlayne.

Dec. 7th. I received some Instances of Divine favour that deserve to be remembered with sincere gratitude, in which I had a sensible and affecting demonstration of the compassionate care of Divine Providence.

Dec. 14th. I continued at home reading Mr. Foster on Morality, and Young's Night Thoughts.

Dec. 28th. We had an eclipse of the Sun this morning. Above one halfe of ye Sun was darkened, but we had a cloudy dark sky and t'was not much darker than usual.

Dec. 31st. In the afternoon there was no preaching at Church, but ye Methodists had a meeting, and many of them joined us after it was over.

1749-50. Jan. 1st. Was called to dine with Mr. Bagshaw and some other friends at Ford, when I received by Mr. Bagshaw an handsome and seasonable present from his Grace the D. of Devonshire, for which I have great reason to be thankful to God. I receive it as a kind and evident answer to prayer.

Jan. 17th. Mr. Hardman and other ministers came to assist us in prayer, on account of the Disease amongst the Cattle.

March 2nd. Dined with the Trustees at the Red Lion at Bakewell. I had a very narrow escape at dinner, in eating part of a big trout. I had a fish hook in my mouth, and was just about to swallow it, but then discovered what it was. And as I was entering Monsal Dale a strong gust of wind blew me and my mare down on one side; had she fallen on the other side I had certainly perished. But thro' Mercy I got safe home in good time but was much harried by ye strong wind full in my face.

March 14th. I was at home all day busy gardening. I sold an heifer to G. Goodwin. We hear ye distemper amongst the cattle is broke out in Rushop, very near us, but hope it is not true.

1750. April 9th. I set out with my grand-daughter Nancy Clegg and Ms Eyre for the Ordination at Derby. Reached Ashbourne about 6 at night, and lodged there.

April 10th. We reached Derby about noon, and dined at the George Inn; son Benjamin came to us from Nottingham.

April 11th. We went to ye Meeting Place about eleven. (62.) We saw at Derby a Rhinoceros and live Crocodile.

April 12th. We set out for home, accompanied with son Benjamin and Mr. Evatt. Ms. Eyre's horse fell with her near

(62). Ordained four ministers, with the usual ceremonies, including son Benjamin.

Duffield, in a deep dirty place. This hindered us at least two hours, but we came to Matlock about 4 in ye afternoon, where Mr. Moult met us, and we all lodged there.

April 13th. We parted with son Benjamin at Matlock Town, and reached Edensor near Chatsworth before noon, and came to Ashford about 3. We dined at Mr. Cresswell's, and came safe home about 8 at night.

April 28th. I am much indisposed by pain in my breast, my stomach I knew was foul and full of flegm and choler, lodged there by getting one cold after another, and drinking too much rum and water in my late journey to Derby; which had also much wasted and sunk my spirits; all which made me apprehend a bad fitt coming on.

June 21st. Mr. Bagshaw sent me this day ten pounds from my kind benefactor ye D. of D.; it was a seasonable supply.

Augst. 1st. (At Manchester.) I visited Mr. Mottershead and old Mrs. Dawson, this day she is 90 years old. I read the news in the Long Room and saw Mr. Berry's gardens.

Augst. 8th. Went to see Mr. Townley's Collection of Sea Shells. Attended De Mainbra's Philosophical Lecture.

Augst. 10th. After dinner I set out with Ms. Eyre for home. We called to drink Tea at Disley, and after being wett with some showers of rain, we came safely home.

Augst. 24th. Called to Timothy Lingard, my tenant; found him dangerously ill of ye Cholera Morbus, gave him about two gallons of chicken broth to be vomited up again, and, at night about 20 drops of laudanum.

Oct. 1st. R. Oldham dined with us, and we walked up to Chappel and diverted ourselves at shuffle-board, and spent ye rest of ye day at Mr. Walker's.

Nov. 14th. Attended ye funeral of a good old friend, Robt. Lowe, of Bradshaw Hall. He was one of our serious, praying Christians, and almost the last.

1750-1. March 6th. I received by the Post my good friend Mr. John Taylor's Treatise on Attonement, which found me delightful employment in reading most part of ye day.

1751. March 29th. In the evening my son James Clegg came to us from Manchester, and brought a Confirmation of the sad tidings of the death of the Prince of Wales. In this the nation sustains a very great loss. May it please God long to preserve ye King.

April 17th.   Was a day set apart for humiliation and prayer, on account of the distemper amongst ye Cattle.

May 5th.   We hear the Princess of Wales is appointed Regent, with a Council of 9 to assist her.   (63.)

June 13th.   A new Election we hear is coming on for a member to succeed ye Marquess of Hartington, who is called up to the House of Lords.   The D. of Devonshire sets up his 3rd son, the Lord Frederick Cavendish, for a Knight of the Shire.

June 14th.   Mr. Bagshaw came over with a letter from his Grace.   Mr. Ash the parson of the Fforest came to us, and we consulted how to secure votes; and I rid out to Bowden Head to secure some there.

June 25th.   Mr. Bagshaw brought me 10 pounds from the D. of Devonshire.

June 26th.   We hear that the D. of Devonshire's son Lord Frederick will be chosen without opposition.

July 3rd.   Ms Eyre set off on my mare to Stockport Races.

Augst. 24th.   I was called again to Mary Robinson, and prescribed for her.   The disease is ye Iliac passion, and the case exceeding dangerous.   I have prayed with her each time I have seen her, and, as God only can help her, I hope it will not be in vain to seek his face and his favour.

Augst. 28th.   I visited the two aged widows at Martinside and prayed with them.

Oct. 3rd.   Had a letter from Mr. Bateman, the Steward, and a call for our Rents.   I got them all up before night and paid them to Mr. Heath, the Receiver of the Land Tax, but by drinking several sorts of liquors, in several companies, my head was disordered.   May ye merciful God pardon my intemperance and make me more careful for ye future.

Oct. 19th.   Last night I receivd from Joseph a barrel of oysters and a pott of British Herrings, an acceptable present.

Oct. 20th.   This day we hear of the death of ye Prince of Orange; he died of a quinzy, a disease I have often been endangered by, yet thro' the forbearance of a merciful God I am yet alive.   This is my birthday.   I have great reason to be deeply humbled and ashamed when I think how long I have lived and to what little good purpose.   God be merciful to me a sinner.

(63).  By the Regency Bill it was provided that in case of the Royal decease before the Prince George should attain the age of 18 the Princess of Wales should be both Guardian of his person and Regent of the Kingdom, but in the latter capacity acting only with advice of a Council.

Nov. 5th.   At night I had the young men who are learning to sing, at supper, and so many more as made up the number 33. Ye singers performed well and all parted well pleased.

Nov. 21st.   At night there was a visible and almost total eclipse of the moon.

Dec. 6th.   Walked up to see a poor woman brought by a pass in a waggon.   She had strong labour pains on her when she was brought, and was delivered ye next day after.

Dec. 9th.   Walked up with Ms. Eyre to see the poor traveller.

Dec. 11th.   Walked up to Chapel-en-le-Frith with Ms. Eyre, and baptized the child of the poor travellers Thomas Philot and his wife ; called it Judith.

Dec. 25th.   I preached in the morning from Heb. 2, 16. Our new sett of singers began to sing in Publick, and some of them dined with me after.

1751-2.   Jan. 22nd.   The storm continues, the carriers cant pass.   There is an universal complaint of want of ffuel, and its our case to be destitute of coles.

Jan. 26th.   As I rid to our Chappel my mare plunged into a snow drift and cast me over her head near the Chappel yate, but, blessed be God, I had not any considerable harm.

Febry. 2nd.   I preached twice from Col. 3, 3, and the Congregation was very full in the afternoon.   There was no service at Church, but many of that Congregation behaved rudely and gave disturbance.

Febry. 19th.   At home all day reading, and writing a long letter to Mr. Taylor of Norwich, on the state of souls departed, and I finished it.

Febry. 28th.   Returned soon to our Chappel to see the new Tomb erected on ye graves of my dear wives.

March 12th.   After dinner I walked up to Town and payed the workmen for the Tombstones.   The price was referred to Mr. Slack, and I paid them all he ordered.   The whole cost, including the carriage, was 3£ 4s. 0d.

March 13th.   We hear there was a terrible hurricane about Stockport.

March 14th.   Last night I was much disturbed with a dream that tidings were come of the death of son Benjamin.   May the Merciful God preserve and spare him !

March 18th. We had much disturbance by Christopher Jow, who came very drunk and gave me the most abusive language, with many oaths and curses.

1752. March 27th. The wife of that old Jow who so lately abused me was here in a poor condition, and in obedience to Christ I relieved her.

March 29th. I preached twice from Acts 5, 30-1, concerning the Resurrection of Christ and his Exaltation, but was not so well prepared as I could have wished.

April 1st. After dinner I was called to John Barns, his wife just delivered of a dead child and in great danger. Thence I was called to a daughter of Will. Grant, our Clark. Thence I rid up to Slack Hall and down to Fford, where I staid too late. I found the rum and water I drank disordered my head when I came out into the cold air, for there was a very cold East wind. I must be more careful to avoid excess for ye future, but I came safe home, blessed be God!

April 12th. I preached both parts of the day from Gal. C, 8, and was much spent at night, and so low spirited as to be scarcely able to perform the duties of our family worship. The Congregation was but thin tho' the weather was good, which gave me some uneasiness. Many young people fall off and go to Church, where they are more at liberty to follow their pleasures, and few parents or masters take any good care of their children or servants, but God can redress all.

May 7th. I was at home til' afternoon. Several came to me for advice, and I gave the best I could, but did not take any fees. God has provided well for me, and all my desire is to do good.

May 10th. I preached twice from Eph. 4, 1. We had a sett of excellent singers from Hatherlow, and I spent a little time with them at ye Inn at night.

May 24th. I preached twice from Heb. 11, 15-16. I went out discouraged by the pain in my leg, and afraid I could not stand, but while I was at my work the pain abated, and continued to do so all day, so that at night it gave me little trouble. What a signal instance is this of Divine goodness, and what abundant cause have I for thankfulness.

July 2nd. There's a collection now on foot amongst us for propagating the Gospel in Fforeign parts.

July 8th. At night Buxton, a tanner of Wirksworth, who makes courtship to Ms. Eyre, came to us and stayed all night, and by ye entertainment she gave him I concluded she shortly intends to marry him, and leave me solitary, which gave me great uneasiness.

July 9th.   Buxton continued with Ms. Eyre all day.

Augst. 23rd.   Last night was the Rush-bearing at Chappel, and in the night some spiteful and malicious persons broke my good yate and carried it into ye brook, and rob'd my garden of a great quantity of fine apples, and either rid or chased my mare til' she lost a shoe, and I was obliged to walk to Chappel, and was much spent and wearied at night.

Augst. 24th.   I was much disturbed in mind on account of Ms. Eyre's intending to leave me, but as I apprehend it may be for her benefit, I determined to submit to it and not to oppose it at all, but to committ myselfe to ye conduct of Divine Providence.

Sept. 14th.   This day the use of the New Style in numbering the days of the months commenceth, and according to that computation the last day of October will be my birthday.   (64.)

Oct. 31st.   Last night Mr. Whitfield preached to great numbers at Chinley End, and this day I hear he is to preach at Glossop.   If his labours conduce to serve the interests of Christianity, and to make his hearers wiser and better, I shall, as I ought, greatly rejoyce.

Nov. 3rd.   My son and several others went out to divert themselves with coursing all day and did not return before night.

Nov. 24th.   The King has arrived in London in health and safety.

Nov. 25th.   I receiv'd a barrel of Oysters and a box of Tobacco from son Joseph.

1753.   Jan. 4th.   At night we had our young men, the sett of singers, to supper, and some others of our neighbours, I think about 30 in all.   They sang many psalms and hymns after, and after prayer most of them returned home.

Jan. 15th.   I was much indisposed all day by ye Hypo: my mind full of darkness, anxiety and perplexity, but I had recourse to God my Refuge and found relief.

Febry. 5th.   Ms. Eyre walked to Slack Hall and Fford.

---

(64). New Style was the alteration of the Calendar ordered to be used in England in 1751, and the next year eleven days were omitted from the Calendar, the 3rd September, 1752, being reckoned as the 14th, so as to make it agree with the Gregorian which had been settled in 1582.   This created much excitement amongst the labouring classes, who thought they had been robbed of eleven days' wages, and who went about in crowds calling out "Gie we back our Eleven Days."

After her return I spake some harsh words to her, which grieved her very much, and I was as much grieved after that I had occasioned her so much trouble.

April 2nd. Ms. Eyre set out for Marple this morning to be married there to S. Buxton some day this week.

April 19th. I was called in the morning to baptize a weak child of John Dean, at Maglow. It was born about three months before the expected time, but the Parents declaring it to have been begotten in lawful wedlock, I baptized it.

May 4th. I took a ride to Cats Tor about an Housekeeper that was offered me; I went to let them know I had at present no occasion for any, having determined to make a trial of my grand-daughter.

May 9th. S. Buxton came for his wife and brought his partner with him. They all dined and drank tea, and then sett off; and very glad I am that she is gone, and that we are parted in peace. Now I hope for peace at home.

May 26th. I paid Mr. Green for 4 gallons of wine.

July 6th. I receiv'd Bayle's Great Historical and Critical Dictionary. It cost me 4 guineas. I spent most of ye day in it.

July 10th. At home til' after dinner, then walked up to town with part of my family to see the Rhinosceros.

Oct. 26th. We had an eclipse of ye sun in ye forenoon, but the skie was cloudy and I could see little of it.

Oct. 31st. Tho. Gee and his brother-in-law Wagstaff brought me an Horse to look at, and I purchased him for 6£ 17s. 6d., and in the afternoon took a ride on him.

Nov. 13th. Visited some children afflicted of the chincough, which has taken off several about us. (65.)

Dec. 4th. I was under apprehensions of dying shortly, and my greatest concern was for ye continuance of ye means of Salvation in these parts after my Decease, but God can provide, and on him I rely With a view to this I have a Ticket purchased for me in the Irish Lottery. If Providence shall favour me with a prize, I have determined that one halfe of it shall be applied to that use or to some other that shall appear more pious and charitable.

1754. Febry. 12th. I found Mr. John Bennet (the Methodist preacher) at my house to return me thanks for my Letter to

(65). Chincough means Whooping Cough.

Sir Henry Houghton on account of which he had the oaths administered to him at Preston, which had been refused to him in this County.

April 12th. I was at home all day reading a book newly published by Dr. Leland of Dublin against ye Deists.

July 20th. Afternoon Mr. Slack came with a message from Joshua Wood, whom I had civilly desired time after time to repair the road that leads to his house, which I was often obliged to pass, tho' it was in such a bad condition that I could not pass without endangering my life. After he had neglected some weeks to repair it, I threatened to have it indicted at the Sessions, upon which he sent Mr. Slack to let me know that he relinquished his seat in our Chappel, and was determined never more to come there. Thus my endeavours to serve yt family in all their sicknesses and to promote their Eternal Salvation above 52 years are requited. This has given me a good deal of uneasiness, but I must endeavour to bear it with patience and meekness, and the merciful God enable me to do so.

July 21st. A crowd of singers came from Motterham to Chappel Church, and many of our young persons had a great desire to hear them, and to oblige them I gave notice at noon that I should begin again at one o'clock, and I concluded the service about three.

Augst. 31st. At night there was in Town a mad revel called the Rush-bearing.

Sept. 1st. In the last night the stone that covered the Tomb under which my wives and three children are interred was thrown off, and a piece broken off, and other mischief done at and about our Chappel. This at first gave me some disturbance, but I prayed for and receiv'd a calmer mind.

Sept. 11th. (At Risley.) We took a ride to Warrington and dined there. Spent most of ye afternoon at Mr. Owens, and in seeing Mr. Pattens fine new built house there.

Sept. 16th. (At Manchester.) Breakfasted at Mr. Mottersheads. Walked to see the Key, called at Mr. Touchets, viewed the books upon sale. Afternoon got a coach which carried six of us to see Mr. Rich. Berry's gardens in Salford. We drank tea there and spent most of ye afternoon. (66.)

Nov. 2nd. This last night the shop of Obadish Porret was broke open by persons unknown and many goods taken out of the looms.

---

(66). The Mersey and Irwell Navigation Canal connecting Manchester and Liverpool was constructed in 1720, and it is probable that the "Key" referred to by Dr. Clegg, was the quay of this canal. There is still an old street in Manchester, near the Irwell, called Quay Street.

1755. Febry. 19th. At night I receiv'd a parcel of Bibles, New Testaments and other good books from Mr. Chandler of London, given by the Society for promoting Religious knowledge among the poor. I am thankful to God for them, and hope many others will have great reason to be so too.

March 11th. The newspapers tell us of very great preparations for war both here and abroad.

July 29th, 1755. (The last Entry. Dr. Clegg died on August 5th, 1755).

At the end of the Diary in another handwriting is the following entry : —

" This Diary is at length come into the possession of Margaret Henrietta Fry Great-Grand-daughter of Dr. Clegg by his daughter Mrs. Middleton. She has been surveying with sincere pleasure the remains of her pious ancestor. May she become a follower of him in faith and practice."

www.ingramcontent.com/pod-product-compliance
Lightning Source LLC
Chambersburg PA
CBHW020807020726
47495CB00008B/2626